FALLEN STAR

And I was alone. An impenetrable barrier of
alcohol and frustration between me and the
nearest human being; an expedition full of
madmen between me and sanity; hundreds
of miles of ice and wilderness between me and
the rest of the world; hundreds of hours of
desolation between me and the future . . . and
north of me a rock slumbered—I could almost
believe it now—millions of miles from the
planet that gave it birth, with the very bones
of Creation frozen at its core. . . .

James Blish

FALLEN STAR

ARROW BOOKS

Arrow Books Ltd
3 Fitzroy Square, London W1

An imprint of the Hutchinson Publishing Group

London Melbourne Sydney Auckland
Wellington Johannesburg and agencies
throughout the world

First published in Great Britain by Faber and Faber 1957
Arrow edition 1977
© James Blish 1957

Made and printed in Great Britain
by The Anchor Press Ltd
Tiptree, Essex

ISBN 0 09 914180 9

For
FIVE
forsan et haec olim meminisse juvabit

I will maintain to my dying day that I never deserved to be handed Jayne Wynn. Of course, I am perhaps the only man in the world she ever met who didn't want her, not even on the rocks, neat. So by the peculiar way my life seems to fall out, I *should* have been the guy to wind up with her. But if I did, it was only for lack of trying.

I never wanted to hold the Earth in the palm of my hand, either; so I got the chance. Naturally; how else could it have happened?

Maybe this doesn't make much sense to you, but it makes perfect sense to me. After a good many years I have become a passionate adherent of the "personal devil" theory of history—modern history, anyhow. I have been through the nineteenth-century evolutionary historians; through Spengler, Toynbee and the other cyclical theorists; through the single-bee-in-bonnet boys like Henry George and Silas McKinley, and just about every other philosophy of history that you can name. That kind of reading helps me to make my living.

And I've come to the reasoned conclusion that only one theory makes sense: the one which assumes that every historical event is aimed personally at my very own head.

It may be paranoid of me, but it works. If there are boats to be missed, I will miss them. If there are picnics to be rained out, I will be there, without my raincoat. If there's a cold going around, I catch it. If I want to go to college in Germany, the country goes Nazi while I'm still in junior high. If I am having a book published on December 11th, war breaks out on December 10th.

These events are not accidental. They are intended to louse me up. They arrive labelled, *Special delivery to Julian Cole*. This explanation passes every test known to science: it is simple, yet comprehensive, and predictions can be made from it. Like this:

As a man whose home base is Pelham, and who regards the territory west of Akron as buffalo country, I should have known that the Committee for the International Geophysical Year would decide to send me to the North Pole. I didn't exactly predict this, but it didn't surprise me, either.

Or: Since I was a science writer in good standing, a full-fledged member of the NASW, making my living selling articles to such journals as *The New York Times Magazine*, *Harper's* and *Scientific American*, it was logical that if the IGY turned up one single epochal *but utterly unprintable* discovery, I would be the guy who had to sit on it. If it involved the whole future of humanity, so much the better; give it to Cole, and don't let him open his mouth.

Now you try it. Given a man thoroughly devoted to his wife, four daughters and defective furnace (there is, they say, something wrong with the pump). Given also Miss Jayne Wynn, spectacularly blonde writer of historical novels as bosomy as herself, reporter for the Middle West's eight-newspaper Faber chain, admired and desired from Korea to Ikurtsk, and the wife of Commodore Geoffrey Bramwell-Farnsworth, R.C.N. Throw in

8

two other women and ten other men, for all the difference that will make. Stir, and put on ice for four months.

That's right. You got it the first time. Of course, personal devil or no personal devil, I balked at it—I balked in spades, and for a while it seemed to be working. As a reward for my stubbornness, I got the unprintable story —and the fate of the Earth, thrust into my flaccid hands like a toy. Since nothing that can possibly happen to me now could be anything but an anticlimax—including being hauled off to Bellevue and being stuffed to the eyebrows with chlorpromazine—I'm going to print the story anyhow. This is it.

And you may call it revenge, if you like.

Book One

I

In January of 1958, Midge and I asked Ham Bloch—
Dr. Hamilton C., the same man who put the luminifer-
ous ether back on the mathematical throne Einstein had
knocked it off of—to our Pelham house for dinner. Ham
is a very old friend of mine, and easily the best friend I
have, but my motives for that evening weren't entirely
social. Ham had recently decided that a fundamental
atomic particle called the anti-chronon ought to exist
(at least, he said deprecatingly, in Hilbert space), and I
was hoping to get him to explain it to me so that I, in
my turn, could explain it to laymen for pelf. It's a nice
way to make a living: you work sitting down, you set
your own hours, and sometimes it seems worth doing—
which is more than you can say for most jobs.

Ham is a very engaging man, with none of the god-
like austerity people associate with physicists. He looks
more like a stevedore, who just possibly may play tenor
sax on the side; and as a matter of fact he is a composer,
though only for fun. Sometimes you can't tell him from
an extraordinary ordinary citizen.

Midge loves him, which I understand entirely and
foster on the rare days when he rubs her the wrong way.
There's nothing peculiar about this, at least by my
lights. I've never felt the least doubt of Midge, and it
goes much deeper than the simple and unrevealing fact
that she has borne me four daughters. (After all, Strind-

berg would have asked, how could I be sure any of them was mine?) It springs from the fact that Midge never looks the same to me two days running. In photographs, and I suppose to other people, she is a small, intense brunette, well-shaped and with good legs which often go unnoticed except at the beach because she goes about most of the time in flat heels and no stockings. She strikes most people, too, as extraordinarily pale and cameo-like—an impression which must be in striking contrast with the way she becomes swearing-excited about the most minor of subjects; she is a great pounder upon flat surfaces, and has sometimes given strangers the notion that she was about to leave me forever because I hadn't had my shoes shined in two weeks. When she is really worried about something, she can screw that classical Italian face into an expression of such intense agony that she seems to be in the thumbscrews—a trick which sometimes makes me want to slap her, if only to give her something really upsetting to look agonized over. (Once I even did, but I won't do it again, believe me.) When she is making love, on the other hand, she becomes stiller and stiller, and when she is truly on the heights her face has the timeless impassivity of a Japanese print.

This mutability, I am convinced, is something that only a happily married man ever sees. Under any other circumstances, women don't differ much from your first impression of them. When I was a little boy just becoming conscious of my sex, I used to wonder why little girls didn't stand looking at themselves in the mirror all day long, enjoying how different they were. I knew why I didn't; after all, I was no mystery to myself. And I felt that Midge, by being different every day, was properly celebrating her different-ness as a woman, which properly should include loving Ham Bloch if he had it coming, as he plainly did. I was equally sure that I was in no danger, for I was sure she knew as well as I did that there was no mystery worth exploring about men.

As it happens, I was never proven wrong about Midge, to my great fortune. But I was stunningly wrong about myself, and about Ham Bloch.

We didn't talk anti-chronons at dinner, all the same, for Midge is bored with technical matters. Her attitude toward all the sciences is that, after all, she can always call somebody. Instead, Ham asked me almost immediately:

"Do you remember Ellen Fremd?"

"Certainly. Dean Howland's wife—a fine girl. Why?"

"Well," Ham said musingly around a mouthful of *risotto*, "she's not Dean's wife any longer, but that's neither here nor there."

"I don't think I know her," Midge said. "Should I be jealous?"

"Twenty-four hours a day," Ham said. "It's the only state of mind proper for a woman. I keep all my wives in a perpetual green funk. Matter of principle."

"If you ever do get married, your wife will probably run you like a railroad," Midge retorted. "But who's Ellen Fremd?"

"She's the official historian of Latham Observatory," I explained. "She wrote that book last year on Latham's six-hundred-foot radio telescope. I met her when she married Dean; I think you met him once just after we were married."

"She's still with Latham," Ham said. "She's also number two editor at Pierpont-Millennium-Artz—handles their Artz Physics series. Right now, she's also on the publications committee for the International Geophysical Year. And she's looking for you."

"Me?" I said, a little squeakily. "I didn't know she cared. Ham, did you put her up to this?"

"I swear I didn't. She just got into town this week, on some business with Artz, and she's going on to Washington on Saturday, on IGY business. She called me yesterday and said straight out, 'Whatever became of Julian Cole?' I hadn't even mentioned your name. She wanted to know if you were still writing science; I told her you never stopped."

I was flattered, and I won't pretend I wasn't. My acquaintanceship with Ellen had been of the slightest, emerging solely out of a deep admiration for her poet-husband—or ex-husband, as it now developed. And Pierpont-Millennium-Artz is *the* name in American scientific publishing; their books get terrific circulation, thanks to an arrangement they have with Pouch Editions, the major paperback house. But at the time I doubt that I even thought about the Pouch tie-in; for once, I wasn't scenting money. I was scenting prestige. Though I had already had several books published, none of them had come from anywhere near so august a publisher.

"What does she want?"

"I think she'd better tell you that herself," Ham said. "I don't mean to be mysterious, I just don't want to suggest more than she may want to offer. But if you're interested in a big, long-term job, she has one for you—that much I can tell you."

13

"You pushed her a little, I'll bet," Midge said.

"Oh, just a little. I think she had Leonard Engel in mind at first, to be frank. But if you're interested——"

"I'm interested," I said promptly. "When do we start?"

Ham grinned at me and polished off his salad before replying. "Why don't you and Midge and I go to see her, say Friday night?" he said at last.

"Not me," Midge said. "That's too soon for me to get a sitter." This was a black lie, since we don't need a sitter; Bethany, our eldest, sits for the other three, and without demur, since she's paid for it. But Ham knew Midge well enough to be aware of how dull she thought all talk about the sciences; he had included her in the invitation *pro forma*.

"Well, it'd be just as well not to make a major engagement out of it, anyhow," he said. "It will have to be pretty tentative. If she gets called to Washington earlier than she expects, all bets are off. But unless you hear from me in the meantime, let's make it for eight-thirty Friday evening."

"Where?"

"Oh, Ellen has an apartment in town; I thought you knew that." He leered at Midge, took out his notebook, and wrote down the address in his spidery mathematician's handwriting, ostentatiously shielding it with his free hand. He tore out the page, folded it once, and passed it to me under the tablecloth.

"Pelham, New York," Midge said darkly. "Dr. Hamilton C. Bloch, noted atom-smasher and home-wrecker, was found here today, partially dismembered. The police, noting the large number of enemies Dr. Bloch had made, reported themselves baffled but not surprised."

"Many screen and television stars, advertising agency receptionists, and other professional beauties are reported to be in mourning," Ham agreed complacently. "A wreath bearing the legend 'To Our Secret Prince', rumoured to be from the entire cast of the Rockettes up to number twenty-four from the left, is already hanging over Dr. Bloch's favourite pencil, which has been placed under glass by the National Society for the Preservation of——"

"I'm going to turn you into an artifact myself in about ten seconds," I said. "Mercy, Ham. My curiosity-bump is killing me. Is this project of Ellen's solely a publishing matter, for Artz? Or does it have something to do with the IGY?"

"Peace," Ham said solemnly. He lit a cigar and pulled on it gently between swallows of coffee. "Let us now discuss the anti-chronon—in hushed voices."

Midge got up. "Excuse me," she said. "I have to put the brood to bed."

I think that Midge did want to go, more or less mildly, to the meeting, if only to get a look at Ellen Fremd; but she didn't broach the subject to me, and by Friday morning it would obviously have been impossible anyhow. A record snowstorm had begun to fall during the night, and was already well on its way toward tying up the entire East Coast; we had eighteen inches in Pelham, and the New York Central train I caught at ten a.m. was the last one to get out of the town until late Sunday afternoon.

As for me, I loathe snow, so probably I should have

seen what was coming—something with *lots* of snow in it. Oh yes, I believe in the pathetic fallacy too; that's the personal devil's favourite trope.

Ellen Fremd's Manhattan roost turned out to be a small, entirely charming apartment in the east twenties, with a high-ceilinged living-room, a miniature kitchen, and a real, functional fireplace toward which I gravitated instantly, dripping as I went. Ham had already arrived, and evidently had tipped Ellen off to my passion for ale. As soon as I was settled by the fire, she brought me a quart of it, with a chilled mug, a bowl of potato chips and another bowl of some spread which tasted like whipped Philadelphia cheese with minced clams and nutmeats in it. (I found out later that it consisted of dehydrated onion soup mixed with sour cream; had she told me that beforehand, nothing could have persuaded me to try it. As it was, I bolted it down most happily.)

We chatted desultorily while I ate and got my bones warm, saying nothing in particular, but re-establishing our lines of communication. As I'd told Ham, I've always thought Ellen a wonderful girl, and she did not seem to me to have changed much. She was noticeably slightly older, perhaps, but otherwise just as always: tall, willowy to the point of thinness but not a gram beyond that point, and with a muted wit that vanishes entirely amongst strangers. She is also quite shy, which mystifies me. Why should a woman with enough brains to be a historian of science, an editor, a Sarton Medal winner and a frequent contributor to *Isis*, and enough looks and grace to pass anywhere for a high-fashion model, be shy with strangers and even with acquaintances?

From where I sat by the fire, I could see that there was a small office just off the living-room. My post gave me a direct view of a magnificent photograph, about four by six, which was hanging over Ellen's desk. It looked like a star caught in the act of blowing up—as, in miniature, it was: the photo was an enlargement from a cosmic-ray emulsion-trace, showing a heavy primary nucleus hitting a carbon atom in the emulsion and knocking it to bits, producing a star of fragment-traces and a shower of more than two hundred mesons.

Nobody with any sense of the drama implicit in a photograph like that—a record of the undoing of one of the basic building blocks of the universe, by a bullet that had travelled unknowable millions of years and miles to effect the catastrophe—could have resisted asking for a closer look. Only afterwards did I begin to appreciate how devious Ellen's shyness had made her. She followed me promptly into the office with a fresh quart of ale, toured me around the room to look at the other pictures —all of them of historic events in recent physics, captured in the traces left by the atomic actors themselves— and had me securely seated at her desk, ready for business, before I had more than half eaten my way through the hors d'œuvres. I suspected that Ham had been through this long before, for he watched me walking innocently into the web with a very small smirk, and took possession of the potato chips and the spread the moment I got up.

Oh, I was a willing victim, I can't pretend that I wasn't. The notion of being entrapped by the number two editor of Pierpont-Millennium-Artz didn't repel me a bit.

"Julian," Ellen said seriously while I opened the second quart of ale, "tell me what you know about the International Geophysical Year."

"That's a sizeable task," I said. "It started July first of last year, and runs to the end of this year, and scientists all over the world are taking part in it; its over-all purpose is to enlarge our knowledge of the Earth; the projects involved range all the way from Antarctic expeditions to the launching of satellite missiles. I wrote a piece for the *Times* about it that pretty well sums up my knowledge of it, except for a few pieces of specialized knowledge that weren't suitable for a lay audience, or were of too limited interest for a general discussion."

"I saw the article. That's what made me ask Ham whether or not you were available. Frankly, the IGY needs competent science writers very badly."

"Well, I'm certainly interested," I said guardedly. "Geophysics isn't exactly my best subject, though."

"That doesn't matter. Just about every science imaginable is involved in the project, and no one writer could cover it all in anything short of a decade. What we need most are historians to cover specific areas of the Year. And we need a man to write two books about the IGY for the layman."

"*Two* books?"

"Yes," she said. "One isn't really about the IGY *per se*; I'll get to that one in a moment. The other is to be published after the Year is over, explaining what we originally hoped to accomplish, and how well we succeeded."

"An official historian, in other words?" Ham asked interestedly.

"No. At least not in the technical sense. The official history will run to a good many volumes, and it won't be for laymen. Probably we'll ask Laura Fermi to do that for us. She has the qualifications, and she seems to be doing a stunning job on the Fifty-five Atomic Energy Conference at Geneva. What we want is an interpreter."

I worked on the ale while I thought about it. It took a good deal of thinking. If Ellen meant to offer the post to me, I couldn't accept it out of hand. It would mean my committing myself to this one project for some years to come, to the practical exclusion of income from one-shot sources—the sources from which, ordinarily, I drew the money to keep a wife, four girls and a draughty fourteen-room house in operating condition.

Finally I decided to say just that, and did. I suspected that Ellen might be a little repelled by the sheer crassness of such an approach to science, but I was wrong.

"I can't offer the whole thing to you anyhow," Ellen said with a faint smile. "Ham reminded me of you——"

I looked a dagger or two at Ham. He blinked benignly at the fire.

"—too late for me to give you still a third book, one explaining what the IGY is for. But I think you may be just right on the second one, the layman's book on what we do accomplish. In the meantime, since the IGY can't pay you a retainer, I've made a tentative arrangement with Artz that will keep you paid until the Year is over."

"Very good. How does it work?"

"Hold on to your bridgework," Ham said sleepily.

"We want you to go with the Second Western Polar Basin Expedition," Ellen said. "You'll act as historian for it, on behalf of the IGY; and after it's over, you'll also write a book about it for Artz. The expedition itself will probably pay you a small salary—we aren't sure about that yet—and Artz will give you an advance on the book. Since you'll be at the North Pole a while, you won't have much need for spending money.

"Now, if you do a good job on the Polar Basin book, I think we'll have no trouble selling the IGY publications committee on hiring you to do the post-Year layman's book. Artz will publish that too; and Pouch Editions will reprint both books. The total sum involved comes to fifteen hundred dollars in advance from Artz, plus four thousand from Pouch, plus whatever Commodore Bramwell-Farnsworth is willing to pay you as a salary. That won't be much, I'm afraid, but it'll at least be noticeable; the Commodore likes to do his exploring in style. Call it sixty-five hundred to seven thousand all told. Could you do it for that?"

"Cripes!" I said feelingly. "I don't know."

"I don't blame you for being cautious," Ellen added. "Considering that the total is conditional. If Artz doesn't like the Polar Basin book, you'd be left with nothing but the one advance and the expedition salary."

"Oh, that doesn't worry me," I said truthfully. "I can handle the job—science writing is my business, and I know I can do it, just like a riveter knows he can rivet. But—the North Pole! I hate winter, Ellen. Let me think a minute. How long would I be away?"

"About four months," Ellen said, smiling, "Bramwell-Farnsworth thinks he'll be ready to leave in late April, and with luck you ought to be back early in September. That isn't so bad—you'll miss the summer, but it isn't like being stuck in Antarctica for two years. But it depends partly on the earth-satellite programme. If a satellite isn't launched successfully by September, you may have to wait for the first successful shot. One of the expedition's purposes is to monitor that shot over the Pole."

"I see. What else will they be doing?"

"Quite a bit. There's a lot we need to know. There'll be fourteen in the party counting yourself, mostly oceanographers; also astronomers, a radiologist, a cryologist, and, of course, a meteorologist."

The roster made sense. The northern ice cap does not lie over a continent, as the Antarctic ice cap does; instead, it's only a sheet floating on the surface of the Arctic Ocean, with no land under it at all. A fully equipped expedition there would need to take daily depth soundings, to record the fluctuations of the ice cap above the ocean bottom—a procedure that would not only yield valuable information for studies of gravity, but might also be a life-or-death matter for the expedition itself, providing new knowledge about the currents in the cold depths, and new knowledge of where crevasses in the cap could be expected to become numerous at various times of the year. The astronomer, of course, would track the earth satellite. The radiologist, working with him, would make cosmic ray observations and study the aurora borealis. The meteorologist would in part be there for the survival of the party itself, but he would also bring back data on the polar weather of immediate practical value to outfits like Scandinavian Air Lines, which run transport routes, and to the U.S. Air Force to boot. The cryologist, I supposed, would be interested both in charting ice movement and in studying the chemistry of everything in sight under conditions of permanent cold.

"It sounds interesting," I said cautiously. "Also somewhat familiar, Ellen. Wasn't there some talk in the papers about this expedition last year? A name like Bramwell-Farnsworth's sounds familiar at any time, of course, but——"

A peculiar expression which I could not then read— a combination, perhaps, of impatience and enforced suspension of judgment—flickered over Ellen's face and was gone.

"They tried to start last year on their own hook," she said. "All kinds of things went wrong; I think they were under-financed. But with IGY support they should be able to get better sponsors this year."

"Why didn't they have IGY support last year?" Ham asked.

"They didn't want it, Ham. We offered it, and they turned it down. They said they'd turn their results over to us after the expedition got back, but they didn't want to follow the programme we'd laid out for them. They had other researches that they wanted to prosecute instead, and above all they wanted to go in 1957, not this year. Now, since they didn't make it last year anyhow, they're willing to go along with us."

"We'll make a Machiavelli of you yet," Ham said. I don't think Ellen understood him; if she did, she gave no sign.

"Julian, what do you think?" she said. "Would you like to try it?"

"Yes," I said. "Midge and the kids won't like it, I suppose. But it sounds to me like it's worth a try."

"Hooray!" Ham said, hoisting his Pilsner glass at me. "Send me back a polar-bear rug, boy. I've got a new young lady who'll settle for nothing else."

Surprisingly, Ellen Fremd blushed slightly and got up abruptly from her desk. I followed her back into the living room, turning over in my mind a few surmises that were both unworthy and none of my damned business—always the most interesting kind. The rest of the evening was pleasant but uneventful, devoted, as I recall, largely to swapping diverting anecdotes about the fabulous Dr. Ralph Alpher.

But when the evening was over and I was ready to venture out into the blizzard again, I astonished myself by blurting out on Ellen's doorstep:

"Ellen, I don't mean to uncover old wounds—I hope you'll forgive me if I do. I only want to say that—that whatever your differences, and they're your own affair —I always enormously admired Dean."

She closed her eyes for a moment, and in the light spilling out the dim hall she looked for just an instant as millennially in repose as that heart-stopping head of Queen Nefertete. Now I had done it; I could have bitten my tongue off. I didn't even know why I had opened my big bazoo.

Then she looked back at me and smiled with the greatest gentleness.

"I admired him too," she said quietly. "Thank you for saying so."

I made my good-byes as best I could, considering the enormity of the gaffe, and the door closed. On the way down the stairs, Ham took my elbow between a thumb and a finger as powerful as wire-cutters.

23

"You bastard," he said. "What a way to return a favour."

"I know," I said. "Right now I'd rather be at the North Pole than anywhere."

"I'd almost rather have you there. You just put me right back where I started from, two years ago."

Then I realized that the favour he was talking about was the favour he had done me, not any of Ellen's.

"I'm sorry," I said. "I didn't mean to. It just happened."

"I know. Maybe it was the right thing to do, for that matter. You couldn't have any conception of how damnably shy she is, especially after the bust-up with Dean; she blames herself."

We paused in the vestibule and looked out at the swirling storm.

"Couldn't you have warned me?" I said. "Hell, Ham, you've been the harem type for as long as I've known you. If you'd said——"

"It's true, I'm my own worst enemy," Ham said, lightly, but with an undertone of bitterness I had never heard from him before. "Well, life isn't all anti-chronons and skittles. Some things have to come the hard way. Let's go have a Tom and Jerry."

He took my arm again, gently, and we plunged blindly out into the still-swirling snowstorm. Ham is the only authentic genius I can count among my friends, but he is more than that: he is a great gentleman. I pay him this tribute here because his role in this story from here on out is both minor and very odd, and I want no doubt left in anybody's mind of what I think of this man. Here

24

he exits, in love, which is as good a going-out as anyone has devised yet.

Midge and the kids didn't like it. Duffy, the four-year-old, was delighted—she spent two nights writing a thank-you letter to Santa Claus for me to carry—until she realized that I wouldn't be coming home from the North Pole every night for supper. Then she wailed like a homeless kitten. I was flattered, but it didn't make things any easier. Bethany, fourteen, took it even harder, to my great surprise; I had thought her too deeply immersed in her universe of cacophony, crushes and crises to notice whether I was home or not. She didn't say much, but suddenly she seemed at least three years younger; she even brought me her math problems, which she had scorned to do as early as ten. Ruth, who is eight, was wide-eyed, and bragged a good deal outside the house, but inside she was preternaturally muted, and abruptly resumed wetting her bed.

This whole complex scared the wits out of me. As for Jeanie, not yet two, there was no possibility of explaining to her what was to come, and that frightened me most of all. A free-lance writer is home and available to his children through most of their waking hours; they are never given the chance to become used to his being normally invisible, as the father who holds an office job usually is. Jeanie saw me almost as often as she saw Midge. What would happen inside her small nascent soul when I vanished into the Arctic for a whole summer would never be riddled. Only this much was certain: when I got back, the baby wouldn't know me any longer.

Had I been weighing these arguments all by myself, I

undoubtedly would have chucked the whole job out of hand. But Midge pressed them, forcing me to think up answers. Answers you invent yourself come to have the force of law.

"I still don't think it's safe," Midge insisted at the end of a long, after-lights-out argument. "Flying over the Pole in an airliner is one thing. But travelling right on the ice, with dog-sleds—that's something else again."

"This isn't Nineteen-nine any longer, Midge," I said. "There'll be nothing primitive or desperate about this expedition. We aren't going there just to be the first men to reach the Pole. That's been done. We're going because there's work to be done up there, work that'll be no good to anybody unless it's brought back, and us with it. There'll be expensive apparatus to protect, as well as lives. Besides, as Ellen says, Bramwell-Farnsworth likes to travel in style. There'll be no real danger."

She sighed faintly and curled up against my back. "All right," she said. "But I still don't like it. At least you won't be leaving for a while."

"No indeed, I don't even know a tenth of the details yet," I said, turning over. "Tomorrow I start to find out."

"All right," she said quietly. "But be sure to come back."

After that, no more was said about it that night.

II

Commodore Geoffrey Bramwell-Farnsworth liked to travel in style.

He was, I discovered at the public library, a World War I Canadian destroyer officer, fifty-six years old, who was now an American citizen; and the Second Western Polar Basin Expedition would be his ninth junket into rough country. The last such expedition, a year-long African safari, had bagged a record-making 2,413-pound rhino, and had explored a great deal of the world's most dismal rain-forest in search of *mokele-mbembe*—the legendary beast which Bramwell-Farnsworth (together with Ivan Sanderson and, more tentatively, Robert Willey) firmly believed to be a dinosaur of the Diplodocus genus.

Well, why not? They never so much as saw *mokele-mbembe*, of course, but had they come back from the Belgian Congo with a live dinosaur, I think few naturalists would have been more than mildly surprised. Since the catching of live coelcanth fishes off the Madagascar coast, almost anything from Africa in the line of "living fossils" seems believable, or at least conceivable; coelcanths are considerably older than dinosaurs, supposedly having been extinct for seventy million years.

For the most part, the safari had been conducted in three ten-ton trailers—one of them carrying supplies and a Diesel-electric generating system, the other two carrying the exploring party in air-conditioned, fluorescent-lighted comfort. The living trailers had full-length bathtubs, too, not just shower stalls; and one of them also contained a well stocked bar.

Nor did Bramwell-Farnsworth have any intention of giving up these rough comforts for the Polar venture. The trailers, somewhat lightened and otherwise converted, had been shipped last year to Alert, 550 miles south of the Pole on the northernmost tip of Ellesmere Island, and presumably were still waiting there for the second try. The newspapers called them his "snow yachts".

Exploring like this is not cheap. The African safari, for instance, had run to $250,000—Bramwell-Farnsworth had apparently mentioned the figure every time he was interviewed—and it was obvious that the Polar Basin expedition would be almost as expensive. This kind of money can no longer be raised as Byrd once raised it, by soliciting pennies from school children—nowadays no school kid would give you a penny toward any destination short of the Moon—nor did the IGY have that much to allocate to what was, from the IGY's point of view, a minor collateral venture. Bramwell-Farnsworth needed other sources of funds, and he had found them.

He was commercially sponsored, like the Mickey Mouse Club, by some eighteen U.S. corporations.

One of them was an outfit I already knew well: Jno. Pfistner & Sons., Inc., a Bronx firm which was the world's largest producer of biological drugs. Though Pfistner was over a century old, they had come into the brand-name pharmaceuticals market only recently, having discovered an antibiotic called tabascomycin which promised to cure everything (to hear them talk) but cancer, the common cold and the divorce rate.

Before this discovery, they had sold their products only in bulk, to other prescription-drug houses, for re-labelling. As a result, they were aggressively publicity-hungry; I could well understand how they had been sucked into this affair.

What I didn't understand was how they were going to justify the money to their stockholders, or explain the tie-in to the press logically enough to make their sponsorship of the venture worth more than a mention ("One of the sponsors of the 'business safari', Jno. Pfistner & Sons., Inc., also contributed medical supplies.") To find out, I went to see Harriet Peters, the Pfistner account exec. at Medical and Agricultural Communications Bureau (ethical division)—which, despite the imposing name, is a public relations agency pure and simple.

Harriet, I found, had come down in the world a little. She had been moved into a much smaller office since I had seen her last, and although she was still as pretty as ever—she was a small, succulent redhead with very white skin, breasts like inverted teacups and a most unbusinesslike rump—she looked rather harried. I knew the signs as of old: Pfistner was thinking of dumping MACB(eth), and MACB(eth) was all set to dump Harriet the moment it happened. I made no comment, however; at these wakes, advance mourning is in bad taste. I told her that I wasn't part of the Press any longer, but that I would be writing a book, and gave details.

"My God," she said, crossing her legs and swinging her foot nervously. "You must be out of your mind, Julian."

"Why do you say that?"

"Well, maybe I'm prejudiced. But from Pfistner's

point of view we've had nothing but trouble with that outfit. It hasn't been anything like worth the work and the money we've put into it—in terms of publicity, I mean."

"Naturally you mean. Tell some more."

"Well," she said judiciously, "I suppose you know that they were supposed to go *last year*. Pfistner gave them five thousand bucks, enough tabascomycin to treat a regiment, two thousand Butamine tablets for airsickness——"

"Why so many for only a dozen people?"

Harriet looked at me with fond pity, as one might look at an idiot son.

"The dogs," she said.

"Oh. Go on."

"Well, they never left the ground, that's all. They got their snowmobiles up to Alert all right, but the take-off was held up for a week by bad weather, and then all of a sudden they were all out of money. The whole thing made them look like fools. And of course it made us look like fools, too; what publicity Pfistner got out of it was three quarters bad."

"Is that all?"

"No, it isn't all, though it would have been enough. They were a terrible nuisance to Pfistner, too—always calling the plant to ask for more money, more drugs, more technical co-operation, making big promises. Bramwell-Farnsworth is a madman, in my opinion, and that bitch of a wife of his is no better. And nothing we could do could persuade him to deal with me instead of the client. He'd agree very sweetly, pat me on the behind——"

"Which you *loathed*——"

"—and ten minutes later he'd be raising Cain with Will Clafflin on the phone, trying to be put through to old Jonathan Pfistner Junior himself. It was a real mess, and I doubt that it'll be any better this year."

"Are you telling this same story to the press?" I said.

"Oh, no, not in those terms—though we are letting it be known that Bramwell-Farnsworth may not get off the ground this year either. He's not going to pull the rug out from under us twice. But since you're planning to go with him, it won't hurt you to go with your eyes open."

It didn't, after all, sound too bad to me. If Bramwell-Farnsworth had been a nuisance to Pfistner, as he pretty obviously had been, it might mean no more than that he was over-zealous in providing for his expedition—hardly a drawback from my point of view. The fact that he was making a second attempt on the Pole was clear enough indication that he hadn't alienated all his sponsors with his first try; after all, he still had Pfistner. I put that one up to Harriet in the form of a short curve over the left-hand corner of the plate.

"Why didn't MACB(eth) recommend against the project this year?"

"We did," Harriet said gloomily. "But 'Once burned, twice shy' doesn't seem to work up in the Bronx on this deal. As a matter of fact, Bramwell-Farnsworth's into them this year for twice as much as last. What could we do? They're the client."

That settled that. Obviously this was all Harriet's headache, and none of mine. I said briskly:

"I guess I'll take my chances. What are we supposed to

do for Pfistner, besides accept their money and use their drugs?"

"Collect soil samples."

"You're out of luck, carrot-top. There's no soil within five hundred miles of the Pole."

"One up, Julian," Harriet said, smiling sweetly. "There's soil within three thousand feet of it. Oceans have floors, remember? When you make your test borings up there, you drop a dredge through the ice and bring up a piece of the bottom. When you bring it home, Pfistner will process it for micro-organisms, and test any that they find for antibiotic activity. On this MACB(eth) hangs a two-page dithyramb on the world-wide soil-sampling campaign that produced tabascomycin, and everybody's happy."

"Very good," I said. "Of course that ocean's been frozen over since the last Ice Age." But it wasn't a good counterploy, and Harriet knew it; bacteria aren't fussy about where they live. Byrd even found rotifers in Antarctica, and rotifers are complex many-celled animals despite their microscopic size.

I got up, stuffing into my jacket the releases and the "backgrounder" MACB(eth) had put out about last year's attempt. "Thanks a lot, Harriet," I said. "I'll carve your name inside a heart on the first glacier I see."

"Better include my phone number. Maybe it'll become an iceberg and all the shipping in the North Atlantic will see it."

Looking-for-another-job type joke. I filed it.

"I'm going to beard my future employer," I said. "Want to come along, or have you seen enough of him?"

"Oh, I'll go. I'm supposed to keep in touch with the

big phony anyhow, and I'd love to see your face when you meet him. Besides, it'll give me something to put on my expense account."

"In that case you can put me on too, and we'll have lunch at Costello's."

"What else?" she said, raising her eyebrows at me.

We had Bloody Marys, Madison Avenue gossip, and London broil for lunch, and I managed to pick up the names of some of Bramwell-Farnsworth's other industrial sponsors. The Harrison Bag Works was supplying him with tents, which were to be lined for insulation with a new vinylidene copolymer film produced by LeFevre Plastics (division of Consolidated Explosives Co., A. O. LeFevre et Cie). The Commodore would pack a rifle made by Parkchester, especially designed for low-temperature operation and lubricated with special low-temperature greases made by Silliputti Chemical Co.; Parkchester and Silliputti authorized him to shoot polar bears with it, and the U.S. Army said that of course if he met any Russians. . . .

The two women in the party were being outfitted by a New York couturier, who would use their pictures and stories in *Vogue* and elsewhere to promote his Snowfire sportswear. Bramwell-Farnsworth and his aides would wear Geneva Jewel chronometers and guide their flight over the ice with Dixon aviation instruments. There was even something for me: one of the snowmobiles included Belfast Tape's newest magnetic dictating equipment.

All this, of course, added up to just the kind of "applied research" that the man on the street thinks of as constituting the whole of science (except, of course, Deep

33

Thinking, like Einstein and the atom bomb). And it was just the kind of "applied research" that Madison Avenue could transform into many column-inches of free puffs for the products involved—free except for what the sponsoring firms had to pay Bramwell-Farnsworth, which was perhaps ten per cent of what the sponsoring firms would have had to spend otherwise on advertising of equivalent value to them. For the likes of Harriet, it was an equitable arrangement all around, and I had no objections. Somebody has to pick up the tab.

But I wondered just how much Ellen Fremd knew about it. The accounting of the expedition's purposes which she had given me in her apartment, the night of the snowstorm, hadn't even hinted at these interlocking commercial commitments. I couldn't quite see how both sets of obligations could be satisfied inside a stay at the Pole of less than four months, travel time allowed. The expedition's photographer in particular was going to have to operate a twenty-four-hour day to get in all the publicity pictures he would be required to bring back, and still have time left over for developing the scientists' pictures and emulsions and making microfilm records for the IGY.

I saw no point, however, in dropping this problem on Harriet's smooth shoulders; she had troubles enough of her own. Besides, for all her ability to handle the vice-presidents of large industrial complexes, and to make attractive and printable the research programmes those complexes sponsor, she was a fluff-head when it came to basic research. She had to be. Basic research doesn't sell products, and public relations is essentially a branch of sales promotion, no matter how passionately people in p.r. deny it.

"Hey!" Harriet said. "You're thinking, you goddam egghead. If you're through ogling me, leave the room."

I grinned at her, flagged one of Tim Costello's incredibly aged waiters, paid the check with the tenner she had slipped me in the cab on the way across town from MACB(eth), and shepherded her out on to Third Avenue, now dazzlingly broad and bright without its El in the February sunlight.

"Where to?" I said.

"The upper West Side." Harriet took my arm possessively. "The Commodore lives high."

And then, for some reason, she seemed to be shivering. I was touched, though I didn't know why. I put my hand over hers.

"Take it easy, carrot-top."

"Onward and upward," she said tautly. "Jason, Jason, bring on the Polar Basin."

"Hush. Here's a cab. Tell me the address."

She tightened her grip on my arm for a moment, and then seemed to relax a little. She said:

"*That's* better, Julian. I love you when you're solicitous. You may pat me three pussy-ant pats on the behind."

"May I?"

After a moment, she said: "You may." But she was still shivering.

III

The first thing that hit me when Jayne Wynn opened the door of the Riverside Drive apartment was that she was naked. This would have been poor observation for any reporter, and particularly for a science writer, since she was in fact more or less fully dressed: an embroidered silk Mexican bridal shirt, plus a tight black skirt which flared just under the hips. But the impression wouldn't quite go away.

"Hello, hello," she said. Both her voice and her smile seemed abstracted. "Oh, hello, Harriet dear. Couldn't you have phoned? The great man isn't expecting you."

"I did phone," Harriet said in a level voice. "And he is expecting us. This is Julian Cole. This is Miss Jayne Wynn, the Commodore's wife."

I said hello rather feebly. The Commodore's wife was twenty years younger than he was, and a familiar enough figure to me from her newspaper and bookjacket photographs; but in the round she was absolutely overwhelming. Tall and long-legged, she belonged to that school of blondes which first became popular as World War II pin-ups: the school whose breasts are as big around as their thighs, or if they aren't, camera angles make them look that big. Since I'm on the short side, and Jayne Wynn's bosom was authentically hypertrophied to boot, her breasts at first struck me as being each as big as her head.

"Julian Cole!" she breathed, as though she were a teen-ager saying "Elvis Presley". She opened the door wide. "I'm delighted to see you, Mr. Cole. We've heard so much about you, and we're so glad you'll be able to come with us. Geoffrey's on the phone, but he'll be with us in a moment. Do come in."

She led the way, ignoring Harriet completely. The poor girl even had to hang up her own hat and coat; the Commodore's wife was far too busy helping me with mine. She disrobed me as if for a royal first night, standing close in a cloud of Polar Passion No. 2 and bumping into me accidentally here and there. I expected unguents from Araby at any moment. It certainly was a hell of a reception for a science writer.

Then she walked before us toward the living room, practising the famous burp-to-the-left, burp-to-the-right walk which had captured her three novel contracts, four husbands (or five, if you count the annulled marriage with the bearded oboe-player who had turned out to be a woman too), and thousands of column-inches of cheesecake photography. All the flexing and quivering reminded me of nothing so much as a muscle-dancer in some Chicago strip joint; these long-boned perpetual adolescents with their irrelevant bulbs are pathetic and desperate creatures.

Remembering that I'd been given permission, I patted Harriet surreptitiously for reassurance. I was relieved to find that she, at least, was in no imminent danger of bursting forth into the world breech first. She was as taut as a contour sheet. *She* didn't remember that she'd given me permission, though. She gave me a furious dig in the ribs with her elbow.

37

The apartment's living room was sizeable and bright. It was dominated by a huge window which looked out over the Drive, the park, and the Hudson toward the Palisades. The furniture was Sloan's Aggressive Modern, and on the wall opposite the window hung a huge Jackson Pollock painting without a frame.

Jayne Wynn sat down on a hassock in an absolute fanfare of legs, and looked brightly at me. "I don't know the Pollock," I said hastily. "What's it called?"

" 'Accidental Number Three'," she said. "It came with the apartment. Isn't it beautiful?"

"It's the biggest Pollock I've ever seen. Almost a mural."

There was a stiff pause, during which Harriet wandered to the window and looked down on the Drive. From somewhere else in the apartment, a very heavy bass voice was rumbling out blurry words, interspersed with almost mechanical frequency with a booming, even laugh, rather like that of a house detective imitating Old King Cole. That, I gathered without straining my brains much, was Geoffrey on the telephone.

"Well," Jayne Wynn said, hugging her knees and looking roguish. "Can I get you something to drink, Julian? We have so much to talk about. Harriet dear, do sit down."

I wanted a drink, all right, but I didn't want to see that torso in motion again for at least the next ten minutes. I was just about to shake my head when the bullroarer in the next room shouted, "NO, dammit!"

"No, thanks," I said, more meekly than I'd intended. The Commodore went back to rumbling his borborygmi, and booming "Oh, ho, ho, ho, ho" every few seconds.

His wife smiled brightly and lifted her heels until they rested against the side of the hassock.

"Well now," she said, with that terribly animated smile. "There's really a great deal to be done. We want you to meet Dr. Elvers, Julian. We hope he'll be here in an hour or so. You'll like him. He's a remarkable man."

I doubted that anybody could be remarkable enough to keep me here a full hour. "Who is he? I don't recognize the name."

"He'll be second in command of the expedition, once it starts. He's a New Yorker with a great deal of experience up north, mostly in Alaska—he's particularly good with sled dogs and he'll be in charge of ours."

"Is he a veterinarian?" I said, puzzled.

"No indeed. He's a licensed physician. He'll be the first doctor ever to set foot on the Pole."

"As a matter of fact," Harriet said from the window, where she was still standing, "he's a chiropodist."

"We're planning to log quite a few 'firsts' while we're at it," Jayne Wynn went on, ignoring Harriet pointedly. "We'll be the first American team to reach the Pole since Peary planted the flag there—that was April 6, 1909. And I'll be the first woman ever to stand on the Pole."

"I may well be the first professional science writer to reach the Pole, for that matter," I said. "If I reach it."

"Of course you'll reach it," Jayne Wynn said warmly, leaning forward and fixing me with her eyes, which were blue and slightly protuberant. "This expedition is going to be a spectacular success, Julian. I've been on a good many with Geoffrey, and I know the signs. Of course, we got quite a bad press last year, through no fault of our own, but I've taken steps to correct that this year." I saw

39

Harriet stiffen; but she said nothing. "That's one of the things I have to discuss with you."

"Why me?"

"Because it will affect what you do. You're the historian for the expedition; I'm its official reporter. We'll have to take steps to insure that our activities don't overlap—or conflict. It would be bad public relations."

This time she shot a feline, sidelong glance at Harriet to see if the shot had told. Obviously it had.

"I don't see why there should be any conflict," I said a little stiffly. "I hadn't figured on filing any stories, not at least until I got back, but if I do they aren't likely to be spot news. I'll be aiming at the science editors— people like Bob Plumb, Gilbert Cant, Earl Ubell, Bill Laurence, Behari-Lal, Dick Winslow. Whatever you file is more likely to be city desk stuff. I'll be sending features, if I send anything."

"There you're wrong, I'm afraid," Jayne said, with an intimate smile. "You see, we don't want any repetition of last year's fiasco. All that ridicule—even outright lies. . . . This time I've contracted with Faber to file *all* the stories that come out of the expedition, with the Faber papers exclusively, over my own by-line. It's the only way we can be *sure* of getting a decent press."

It didn't look like such a sure thing to me, and it brought Harriet from the window in a hurry.

"You can't do that, Jayne," she said indignantly. "You must be out of your mind. There are eighteen big corporations in on this, and nearly every one of them has some sort of public relations project tied to it. How are you going to keep them from sending their own releases to the papers? You can't even protect your exclusives."

"I think I can, Harriet dear. All I have to do is see each story that the p.r. people propose to send, and get it first to FNS under my own by-line. After that, your agency and the others can release it for general pick up."

"That won't work. We can't 'release' a copyrighted exclusive."

"Then make changes, dear," Jayne said airily. "That's what you people are paid to do—put the commas in the right place."

"Nonsense. Superficial changes don't invalidate a newspaper's or a wire service's copyright. And if we write a whole new release instead, we'll have to clear it through you and the problem is as bad as it was in the first place. I can just see Pfistner sitting still for that system. Let alone a cartel, like LeFevre. Which side do you think your bread is buttered on, anyhow?"

Jayne was obviously very close to losing her temper; only the fact that Harriet had already lost hers had kept the older woman in control of herself this long, as far as I could see. Since the problem obviously was insoluble unless one of them gave way completely—it was that kind of problem, either Jayne kept her exclusives or she relinquished them, there was no middle course—the argument could well have gone on indefinitely. Inevitably it would have involved me, since I thought Harriet in the right, and Harriet wouldn't have hesitated to ask me for support.

Luckily, at this point Geoffrey Bramwell-Farnsworth erupted into the room.

"Well, well," he said in his booming bass voice. "Hello, Harriet, nice to see you; sorry to be tardy. And, you, sir; welcome, I'm Commodore Farnsworth."

41

I stood up and introduced myself; Jayne was too busy glaring at Harriet. The Commodore's handshake was powerful, but not deliberately bone-crushing—which was a good thing, for he could have ground bones if he had wanted to. He was a huge man, at least six feet four, with a figure almost as exaggerated as that of a keg sitting on a camera tripod. He didn't have three legs, of course, but the two he had were long and relatively slender, and his hips were narrow too. His trunk and chest, however, were enormous, and it was impossible for me to see both his shoulders at once while I was standing at handshaking distance. His head was the bullet dome of the Prussian or Scandinavian, on a thick neck, reminding me instantly of the familiar bust of Spengler; his hair was fire-red except for the grey at the temples, and in the middle stages of regrowth from a crew cut, rather like a shaving-brush which had been set afire. He was a most peculiar physical type, suggesting instantly that his glands must have been—and might still be —considerably out of whack: the bullet head, generally a product of sexual precocity, at war with the long extremities of delayed adolescence, the huge hands and feet and the prominent bony ridges over the eyes obvious stigmas of early acromegaly—a real endocrinologist's nightmare. Without foreknowledge, I would have said he was forty.

But I bring this up only by hindsight. At the time, I believe, I noticed only that he was big, and that he was wearing the button of the Explorers' Club in the lapel of a white linen dinner-jacket.

"Glad to meet you, Julian," he said warmly. "Quite a party we're going to have. Forty days at the Pole—the busiest forty days in exploration history, I'm going to see to that. Jayne, these people have no drinks! What's yours, sir?"

"Scotch if it's available," I said gratefully. I had no objection to being waited upon by the Commodore, and I wanted the drink.

"Of course it is, of course. Harriet, a bit of Gin and It, eh?"

"Fine, Geoffrey." She was smiling, I noticed.

"I suppose Jayne's been filling you in," he said from the sideboard. "Sorry to have missed it. Arguing with suppliers—sometimes seems to take up the whole damned day. Arguing about credit, if you can imagine that—with *our* blue-chip backers? I say shame, then I say *Schade*, then I say *vergogna*, and then I just yell at 'em. I'm a good yeller." He grinned and handed me my drink. "Usually it works."

I grinned back. The fact is that I liked him at once. He had a tremendous magnetism, and I was happy to find he had a sense of humour to go with it, and could deprecate himself in front of strangers. There was no doubt that he was deliberately flamboyant; it stuck out all over him. But then, Byrd had had more than a touch of the grandstander in him, too—which had simply been the icing over an essentially brave and serious-minded man. Who's perfect?

"Forty days doesn't seem very long to me," I said, after a long, grateful pull of exceptionally good, smoky Scotch. "Between your commercial commitments and all the observations the IGY needs——"

"Julian, let me tell you that the IGY is at the very bottom of my priority list," he said, sitting down in a

43

heavy armchair and hitching it closer to me with one hand. "I didn't want this expedition to be an IGY project from the beginning; it was forced on me. I made that very clear to everybody, from Kaplan right on down, last year. They think that they're forward-looking and adventurous and God knows what else because they're going to send up some satellites during the Year—after the American Rocket Society kicked them repeatedly into doing what should have been done ten years ago. D'you know the kind of interplanetary data *I'll* be looking for? No, of course you don't. I'll tell you. It has nothing to do with whether the Earth is thirty feet bigger around the middle than we thought it was. What good is the Earth? What *I* want is a piece of Planet Number Four-and-a-half."

He had me there. The fourth planet, of course, is Mars; Earth is the third, counting outward from the Sun. The fifth is Jupiter. But four-and-a-half? It didn't exist. The space between the orbits of Mars and Jupiter is an endless elliptical river of cosmic junk, made up of rocks of all shapes and sizes. There are thousands of them; the biggest is some five hundred miles in diameter, the smallest may be no bigger than pebbles; the average size is about that of a free-floating mountain. These little nuisance-worlds are usually called "asteroids", but they are not stars and have nothing in common with stars; "planetoids" is a better term.

"Four-and-a-half?" I said incredulously. "You expect to find an asteroid at the North Pole?"

"I expect nothing, Julian. An explorer learns to have hopes, but no expectations. I think that the asteroids all belonged to a single planet once; and that it exploded

44

not so long ago. I hope to find evidence of that at the Pole—evidence that will nail the hypothesis right down into known fact."

"Why at the Pole particularly?"

He leaned forward and gazed earnestly into my face. Evidently Jayne's similar and overwhelming approach had been copied from him, with the slight modifications necessary to take fullest advantage of deep decolletage. The notion that *he* had copied it from *her* was out of the question; compared to him, she was a palimpsest subject to anyone's erasure and inscription.

"Look at it this way," he said. "We *know* that some sort of a break up occurred out there. There used to be a larger body between Mars and Jupiter. Now it's gone, and there's nothing left there but thousands and thousands of rocks. Some of those rocks enter our atmosphere as meteors; usually they burn up before we can study them, but some that we have analysed show that they were recently part of a much larger body. Are you with me so far?"

I was, more or less. I dimly remembered some papers in *Nature* which had suggested something of the sort. But it was based on highly disputable evidence, as I recalled; Whipple and other experts still stuck to the hypothesis that almost all meteors are the debris of comets. I said so.

"Whipple's got to be cautious, he's an astronomer with a reputation to protect," the Commodore said. "I'm only an explorer. If you want a scientist who supports my position, I'll give you Urey. But let's not pair off experts. Why, man, the bottom of every ocean in the world is littered with minute round grains of iron, and *everybody* agrees that those came here from space, and that they had to be the result of the break up of the asteroidal planet. They're even called 'cosmic granules' in the literature. Isn't that so?"

"I think it is."

"Very good. Now the granules are too small to tell us anything much, and the meteors get such rough treatment when they pass through our atmosphere that it's hard to agree on what analysis of them shows. But the granules and the meteors are still falling. They're late products of the explosion. What happened right here on Earth immediately after the explosion—only a few million years ago? What a dusting we must have gotten then! What a bombardment! How else do you account for Meteor Crater, Chubb Crater, the Carolina potholes? And then came the last glaciation—and of all the seas, only the North Polar Sea has been capped with ice ever since! Doesn't that suggest anything to you, man?"

"Not very much, I'm afraid."

"I'm disappointed in you," he said solemnly. "Suppose a really big fragment of that protoplanet—big enough to get through our atmosphere with only its skin burned off —wound up at the bottom of the Arctic Ocean. Then the ocean froze over. There can't be any recent dust or fragments on the floor of that ocean. And what fell a few million years ago has been resting there under constant refrigeration, so chemical changes in it would be at a minimum; and physical wear-and-tear from thermal currents, exfoliation and so on has had no chance to destroy the evidence it contains. Why, man, *anything* could be down there in that deep-freeze. And that's what *I* want to look for; I'm not interested in the IGY's

46

piddling little satellites. It's a whole planet I'm looking for!"

It was an impressive notion, all right. But it still didn't convince me, except as a notion—something for a science-fiction writer to play with. After all, if there had never been any protoplanet between Mars and Jupiter— and as I recalled, if there had been, the bottom number of such planets had to be three, and the probability was that there had been scores—then any granules and meteorites the Commodore found under the Arctic ice-cap would be just like those everybody else already had under study.

As a research project, competing with all the others for a chunk of our forty days at the Pole, it wasn't a fortieth as important as the IGY satellite programme. We *knew* what we were likely to get out of that.

"I see it doesn't inspire you," the Commodore said, taking my glass away for a refill. "But it will, it will. You need imagination in this exploring trade, Julian."

"Like *mokele-mbembe*?" I ventured.

"Exactly, exactly!" He seemed genuinely pleased. "You must look for the possible. Never mind that it's also the unlikely, as far as the rules of evidence are concerned. Suppose you never find it? You cover a lot of territory while you're looking; isn't that so?"

"It certainly is," I said. "I still don't much credit the idea, but I endorse the principle. And at least you'll dredge up Pfistner's soil samples in the process."

"Oh, yes," he said. "That's a part of the programme that intrigues me too. It isn't even certain that there's any life down there at all. If there is, I doubt that Pfistner will ever get an antibiotic out of it; competition

47

between micro-organisms can't be very keen at those temperatures. But in the antibiotics business, where there's life there's hope, I should think."

Harriet was watching me with an expression of virulent disapproval, but there was nothing I could do about that. What the hell; I *liked* the guy. And I think he could sense it. Underneath his flamboyance, he seemed to be in search of approval—not at all an uncommon thing in adventurers of all kinds. And obviously he warmed to even the slightest show of it, as though he was genuinely ignorant of how hypnotic his vitality alone could be to a new acquaintance.

"Geoffrey," Jayne said, putting her hands behind her and leaning back on the hassock to look up at him. The pose was as deliberately provocative as any press agent could have asked, but Farnsworth frankly didn't notice. "Show Julian our aeroplane."

"Oh, the plane!" he said enthusiastically. "Now there's a whale of a piece of apparatus. It's been out of service for years—nobody wanted it—but it's still airworthy and it's perfect for Polar operation. Let me see, where are those pictures? Rupert Hawkes built it as a prototype for the Air Force, but they had bad luck with it, and it was their own fault. The first thing they did—Jayne, what did I do with those pictures?—was to build another one twice as big, and of course it was unstable; turned turtle on its first flight, killed a damned good test pilot who didn't want to have anything to do with it in the first place. But the prototype—ah! here they are—is a perfectly stable medium transport, and the Air Force has given us the use of it. Here it is, sir. The Hawkes Flying Tail—a bizarre aircraft to be sure, but incredibly capacious, and with enormously high lift—just the thing for low-temperature flying. I'm going to pilot it myself, and I am *not* a reckless pilot."

I looked at the pictures, at first with flat incredulity, and then, gradually, with dawning recognition. It had been years since the Hawkes Flying Tail had dropped out of the publicity limelight, and since nothing like it had ever been flown since, let alone adopted into mass production, I had almost forgotten that such a thing had ever existed. It looked like nothing so much as a powered boxkite, or—as the newspapers' name suggested—the tail of an ordinary aircraft detached, enlarged, slightly redesigned, and put into the air on its own.

None of the photos Farnsworth had given me showed it in flight, though presumably Hawkes had flown it; but Hawkes has flown everything, and is alive today only by virtue of multiple miracles, like all the Quiet Birdmen who survived the barnstorming era. To me, the Flying Tail looked in Farnsworth's photos to be about as airworthy as a child's jack, for all its massive size.

And I was going to be flying to the North Pole in that crate. Of course it was airworthy if the CAA had granted it an airworthiness certificate—but I noticed that it bore an X-series licence number on its airfoils, meaning "experimental", which meant the CAA would consider it airworthy until events proved it otherwise. I was not reassured.

"Is this the plane you got to Boston in last year?" I said.

"No, we couldn't get it certified in time. Last year we flew a C-Forty-Seven—a flying boxcar. But I've taken this plane up. She handles very well once you get used to her; the main problem is in landing, because of the odd configuration. I don't anticipate any trouble."

I didn't anticipate any *specific* trouble either. But I had a hunch that a man who invariably gets kicked when he bends over to pick up a ten dollar bill had no business boarding the Hawkes Flying Tail, not even on an inspection tour.

"I'm afraid Dr. Elvers isn't going to make it," Jayne was saying. "It's too bad. We did so want the two of you to meet."

"There'll be another time," the Commodore said abstractedly over the pictures. Jayne's remark, however, reminded me that it was getting late. I looked at my watch.

"Oh, oh," I said. "If I'm going to catch my train home, I'll have to hump for it. Thanks very much for the drinks. I'll be seeing you again shortly, of course. When is the take off scheduled for?"

"Monday, April twenty-ninth," Farnsworth said. "Glad you're going with us, Julian."

"I'm sure your scientific training will be a great asset," Jayne said, uncoiling, and giving me a glowing smile of a kind I have never before seen bestowed on scientific training.

"I'll go along with you," Harriet said.

And she did; and so I missed my train after all. Harriet insisted that we stop off in a bar for another drink, and since I was indebted to her, I couldn't very well refuse.

"You can catch a later train," she insisted. "I want to talk to you."

Once we had our drinks, she came at me directly. "Are

50

you really going to go along with that big blowhard?" she demanded.

"It looks that way," I said. "I'll admit that I see a few drawbacks I hadn't seen before. I don't like the looks of that aircraft one bit. And Jayne rather alarms me, too. But on the whole I think the Commodore's rather likeable. And the expedition's worth while, after all."

"That I don't see at all. It's just a grandstanding stunt. Him and his asteroids."

"The asteroids are at least harmless, and he might even be on the right track. And the IGY seems to think the expedition will be valuable."

Harriet scowled into her drink. "What is this IGY, anyhow? I keep seeing stuff about it in the papers, but I never did find a coherent account of what it's all about. Is it just this artificial satellite business Ike announced in '55?"

"No, there's a lot more to it than that. The period itself runs from July 1st, 1957 to December 31st, 1958. Essentially it's a world-wide co-operative study of the Earth itself. Geophysics covers the land, the atmosphere, the oceans, and all the things outside the Earth that affect it—the sun, for instance, and cosmic rays. During the Year, the scientists are concentrating on fields of study that require simultaneous observations to be made all over the world. I can't give you the whole list—it keeps growing constantly, anyhow—but some of the problems they're tackling are the aurora borealis and the airglow, the magnetism of the Earth, its gravitational field—let me see—glaciers, and the weather, oceanography, earthquakes.... I forget the rest, but it's a large order. There's a rocket programme for studying the upper atmosphere, and of course the satellites—they ought to yield all kinds of basic information."

"I can't quite picture the Commodore as part of a vast fellowship of dedicated basic research men," Harriet said gloomily. "But I suppose it takes all kinds. I was hoping you'd see through him, and give me some ammunition for separating him from his Pfistner sponsorship. I can't do it by myself, I've proven that. But you let me down."

"Sorry, carrot-top. He's peculiar, but I think his expedition is worth while. Otherwise I'd be backing out of it as fast as ever my little legs could run."

"Well, the least you can do is to see me home."

I had had just enough to drink so that the idea tempted me, but I didn't need much Super-Ego to see what my personal devil would make of such an opportunity. I backed out, ungraciously but fast.

I was half-way back to Pelham on the 8.35 before I realized that I had completely forgotten to ask the Commodore about salary.

IV

Just to be on the safe side, I called Ellen Fremd the next day and gave her the meat of Farnsworth's pet idea. To my surprise, she was interested, though she showed her usual intellectual caution.

"I think the chances are very much against his finding anything," she told me over the phone. "The whole idea of an asteroidal protoplanet is speculative. It's just as likely that the asteroids are the debris of a planet that failed to form in the very beginning, because the mass of Jupiter kept scattering the components. But there is this recent work on the helium content of meteorites; that's what you saw in *Nature*. It suggests that certain types of them were molten only a few million years ago, and that they weren't exposed to space at the time. It's difficult to understand how that could be possible, unless they were part of some quite sizeable solid body back then."

"Frankly, Ellen, you flabbergast me. I thought the idea was a fugitive from a science-fiction story. If Farnsworth did grapple up a big chunk from the ocean bottom up North, would the IGY be interested in it?"

"Certainly," Ellen said. "As a matter of fact, at least two of the projects on the satellite Flight Priority List have a bearing on it. Let's see if I have the list here. . . . Yes. There's ESP-4, measurement of interplanetary matter, under Maurice Dubin at Cambridge; and ESP-7, measurement of meteoric dust erosion of the satellite skin, under Singer at the University of Maryland. So if Farnsworth finds anything that leads us to alter our current ideas of meteor density in space—as any data tending to support the protoplanet hypothesis would do—we would be most interested.

"Of course," she added thoughtfully, "the Arctic Ocean isn't heavily iced over, as most people seem to think. And Farnsworth's notion that it's been ice-covered ever since the end of the Pliocene is possibly a little simplistic. After all, the last Ice Age ended less than 11,000 years ago. Anyhow, Julian, it's well worth looking into, I think."

I thanked her and hung up, feeling a little dizzy. I was not in spectacularly good shape anyhow, thanks to a protracted argument with Midge which had lasted for three quarts of ale after I had gotten home the previous night. I think Midge might have passed over my new association with a Notorious Woman like Jayne Wynn, or my being much too late for dinner without having phoned, or my having been out drinking with Harriet. The combination, however, was too much for her. The argument was dull and lengthy, as are all arguments which are essentially about nothing, and the end-product was one of those awful hangovers which fill the whole of the next day with an inexplicable sense of guilt and impending disaster, like the first intimations of schizophrenia. Indoles in the blood, I suppose.

But I couldn't go back to bed today, all the same. There was still too much that I didn't know.

The first thing I wanted to do was to get out to Teterboro and get my own personal look at the Flying Tail. Somewhere during the day I had also to repair my omission to ask the Commodore about salary, too. But the aircraft came first.

Getting to Teterboro from Pelham, since it involves going through Manhattan, is much more difficult than going from New York to Chicago, but I made it by two in the afternoon. I showed my credentials to the Port of New York Authority administrator who runs the airport, and went out to look for the Hawkes Flying Tail.

It wasn't there.

I couldn't see any place on the field where such an object could be hidden. I went to the nearest hangar, which turned out to belong to the Peterkin Flying School; a mechanic told me that Peterkin was out with a student, but would be down soon. After a while a Piper Tri-Pacer which I had seen circling the field at about 800 feet came in for a landing and taxied toward us.

"Sure, I know the ship you mean," Peterkin told me. "She's been sitting off in this corner of the field since about 1942. Old Squats, we called her. Every so often the Air Force would tune her up a little. Then they'd fill up her fuel tanks and leave her again."

"Why'd they fill her up?"

"Corrosion," Peterkin said, with the superiority of the flier for the groundlubber. "If you don't keep tanks full, they corrode. Water condenses on the inside."

"Oh. Well, where is she now?"

"You got me," Peterkin said. "All I know is, a bunch of characters in green uniforms came over here last week and inspected her from top to bottom. Then they came back about three days ago and took her off, without even anybody checking 'em out in her. She hasn't been back since. Funniest looking thing in flight since birds."

55

Green uniforms? I hightailed it back to the operations office.

"Why, sure," the operations officer said. "It was all perfectly in order. She was sold to the Venezuelan Air Force, and they came and got her, that's all. They didn't need to be checked out in her, since she was an X Model; I don't know who'd be qualified to check a pilot out in her anyhow, except maybe Rupert Hawkes."

"My boss flew it," I said. "Commodore Bramwell-Farnsworth."

"Oh," the operations officer said, "him. I saw him do it. He may be hell on wheels in a Ford Trimotor, but I wouldn't send my worst enemy up with him in that ship. Half the time he was flying her upside down." He thought a moment and then added, "It *is* a little hard to tell which side is supposed to be the upside."

"This is going to cause a whale of a stink," I said. "The Air Force gave the use of that aircraft to the Commodore. He's supposed to fly it on a North Pole expedition at the end of April."

"Well, he's lucky," the operations officer said. "He wouldn't have gotten Old Squats as far as Boston. Even Chuck Yaeger wouldn't fly that plane."

I regarded the reference to Boston as singularly unfortunate, but at least the Commodore wasn't around to hear it.

"Look," I said. "This has got to be a clerical error of some kind. The Air Force can't give two different outfits the same aircraft. Maybe the Venezuelans don't have title yet; can't you call them back until this thing's settled?"

"How can I do that? It doesn't take all year to get to

Venezuela. They must have landed in Caracas the day after they left here, at the latest. She's probably flying bananas by now. If your boss still wants her back, he'll have to take it up with the Air Force—it's out of my hands. As far as I'm concerned, the kids had all the proper papers, they had a right to Old Squats, and they took her away. I'm glad to be rid of the old eyesore."

I didn't know what to think. I hadn't been eager to ride in the Flying Tail, but I didn't want to be part of a grounded expedition, either. I retired in confusion to the bar, and thence to a phone booth from which I called Harriet at MACB(eth). She wasn't in the office and the receptionist couldn't say when she'd be back; was there any message? I left a message, and began wending my sweaty way back to Pelham. This was going to be a nasty piece of news to have to break to the Commodore, and I wasn't going to break it to him without prior consultation with someone who knew him at least a little better than I did. I have many defects, but there's one good thing you can say about me: I'm a genuinely thorough-going coward.

I was playing roll-the-ball with the baby after dinner when Harriet called. Midge's expression as she transferred the phone to me was one impossible to describe to bachelors; it was, well, tentatively grim. I put on the standard answering expression, Righteous Reproof No. 2, and said: "Harriet?"

"Hello, Julian," Harriet's voice said dolefully.

"Oh. Hello. You sound like the North Orange Crematorium. I gather that you got the news."

"Noose? How did you know? I was just told today. This afternoon."

"You got it the easy way. I had to hunt for it."

57

"Hunt for what?"

"The gawdam aeroplane, what else?"

"Julian," Harriet said. "What aeroplane? What are you talking about?"

"I'm beginning to wonder. Let's start over. Hello, Harriet. What's new?"

"I've been fired."

I groped for a chair, caromed off the piano with a noise like a Reader's Digest condensation of a Roger Sessions symphony, and wound up perched on a corner of the piano-bench. "Cripes, Harriet."

"Well, I'm bearing up bravely. Actually I'm not fired yet. It's just that Pfistner dropped MACB(eth) today, and I got two weeks' notice. But I've got to start hunting. You know how it is for a woman in this game."

I did. I said, "What are you planning?"

"There's not much I can do. I've got to use the only solid contact I have. That's the Commodore, damn his golden hide. If you'll help, maybe he'll take me on as publicity gal for the expedition."

I wormed my bottom off the corner of the bench on to the edge and just breathed for a moment. Considering the multiple drawbacks such an arrangement would have for Harriet, it was hard to imagine why she could even entertain it. But then, I didn't know how badly off she really was; in her own mind she had already fallen from the high Miltonian heaven of being a "public relations counsel" to the dismal universal hiss of "publicity", at least inside her own carefully coiffed skull. I didn't underestimate the length of that fall, imaginary though it usually seems to the people who do the useful work of the world.

"What would you like me to do?" I said cautiously.

"Well, maybe you can give me a few extra assets to offer, outside of my experience and so on. The Commodore needs names with scientific status to put on his letter head. If I could bring him somebody like Robert Willey; not to go with the expedition, but just to act as technical adviser or something. . . . What do you think?"

It was feasible, of course. Robert Willey was an old acquaintance of mine, though I couldn't properly describe him as a close friend. He is widely known to the public as an expert on a strange assortment of subjects, chiefly rocketry, natural history and structural engineering, about all of which he has written some notably informative and charming books. He is, in addition, the author of innumerable popular magazine articles, and is a lecturer with more bids than he can possibly fill.

Though he is no longer a practising scientist, the public thinks of him as one—an impression aided by his record as a pioneer in the first German rocket society, his expulsion by the Nazis, and the many times he is cited as an authority by other science writers. He would be an undeniable asset to the Commodore, even if only as a name on a letter head.

"I'll tell you what," I said. "I can't deliver Willey to you on a platter; you'll have to approach him yourself. He's a busy man, and he'll make up his own mind whether or not he's interested in our Arctic cruise. You'll find his phone number in the Queens book. If you catch him in town, explain the expedition to him and ask him if he's interested. You can use my name, which he'll probably remember without any trouble, and you can also tell him that this is an IGY-sponsored project. But bear in mind that if he *is* interested, Farnsworth will have to pay for him. Willey makes money every time he opens his mouth, and the arrangement satisfies him perfectly."

"I'll remember," Harriet said. "Thank you, Julian." She sounded very humble; only then did I begin to realize what a shock she had had.

"Don't be jittery, Harriet. He's really a very gracious, generous guy, though his accent makes him sound gruff. It's just that he makes his living from his name, so he's not going to give it away. You'll have to ask Farnsworth whether or not he wants Willey enough to pay him; then you go ahead and phone Willey. Okay?"

"I see. Another version of the old Army game. I've played that often enough with clients. Thanks, Julian; I'll let you know what happens."

"You can do better than that," I said. "Call the Commodore right now and tell him he has no aeroplane."

I explained swiftly what I had found at Teterboro. Somewhere in the background I could hear the baby borne off to bed, crying, "Daddy, ball, daddy, ball" in doleful protest. I wish I'd been listening more closely. Instead, I added:

"I must confess that I've got no stomach for the job, which is why I'm asking you to do it. But the faster it's done, the better. He'll need the news right away, so he can start hotting up the wires to Washington. Maybe you know him well enough to make him realize you're doing him a favour—and you can mix the Robert Willey angle in with it."

"Sure I can. From my point of view it's a break. Julian,

60

you're an angel—a frigid angel. Good-bye, I've got to warm up my broomstick."

"Go to it, carrot-top."

I hung up. Behind me, Midge said, evenly: "*Carrot-top*, Julian?"

And off we went again.

V

The Commodore worked prodigies with Washington; evidently he was highly regarded there, at least in some quarters—and of course the expedition had had a quasi-official status. There was, however, nothing that the Air Force could do about the Flying Tail. Through some kind of intradepartmental bollix, that had been sold fair-and-square to the Venezuelans, and it couldn't very well be unsold. But there was an existing commitment to the Commodore which the AF was quite willing to recognize.

We wound up with the use of two B-29s in fair condition—though only one was pressurized. Perforce, the dogs would ride in that one, it being impossible to put oxygen masks on dogs. Nor would Dr. Elvers, whom I had finally met, wear well under that kind of treatment: he was a small, dried prune of a man, with snow-white hair and pink-rimmed eyes. To my surprise, Farnsworth promptly appointed Jayne the captain of the unpressurized craft, which would also carry Sidney Goldstein, our cryologist; Ben Taurasi, our engineer-mechanic; Harry Chain, our radioman; Fred Klein, our geologist, and Marshall Benz, our oceanographer—exactly half of our total personnel.

As a sort of bonus (which is Washington past-tense Latin for "boner"), the Air Force also made us several concessions. Chiefest of these was their designating us an official AF mission. Aside from giving us unquestioned access to AF installations in the North, what this meant in practice was that after we had gassed and oiled up the big planes at our own expense, we could bill the government for the taxes. This didn't put any money back into Farnsworth's pocket before the expedition started—and I had already seen enough of his operation to realize that lack of ready cash was chronic with him except when it was acute—but it made his credit good at Teterboro, which was almost as satisfactory.

Nevertheless, Farnsworth was far from satisfied. The delays and setbacks he had suffered over the past two years had slowly begun to convince him that Somebody was out to get the expedition. He had no hypotheses about the identity of this Somebody, which at least made him an unusual sample of this kind of crackpottery— almost anybody else would have been blaming the Reds, the Pentagon, or some other whipping-boy—or about what Somebody might hope to gain by lousing us up. All the same it did no good to ask pointed questions. On this subject, it was better to ignore Farnsworth as completely as possible.

We had an early spring in '58, as I'm sure you'll remember. The increasingly warm days were forcible reminders of how short the time was growing before take off. As the interval shortened, press interest in us heightened, and Harriet took every possible advantage of that interest. She arranged interviews right and left; the Commodore was given the chance to radiate animal magnetism over three high-rated network TV shows, a whole battery of newsreel shorts, and radio interviews galore—to say nothing of the magazine pieces that were written about him. All this was in addition to the stuff the papers were carrying.

It was a much better p.r. showing than Jayne could have brought off. It's one thing to be an experienced newspaper-man or woman, but it's quite another to be an experienced publicist, and Harriet was proving it to the hilt. I am unable to say that Jayne was much warmed by the demonstration.

But it pleased the expedition's sponsors; when the headlines began to refer to us as "2WPBE" instead of "POLAR TRY", they almost wriggled with delight. And it pleased the Commodore to the very verge of disaster. On a higher and more cerebral plane, Robert Willey did a marvellous job of explaining to the public what we were going to the Pole for, giving us a good coating of scientific prestige. The Commodore had agreed immediately to paying Willey's asking price, a piece of farsightedness on his part that I hadn't really expected.

As for my salary, that had also turned out to be generous. That is, the Commodore paid me exactly what Ellen Fremd had forecast, which, now that I knew him better, I had to regard as generous. The cheques were not, however, always forthcoming on paydays. Farnsworth finally settled down to being steadily one week behind on my cheque.

The public relations agencies of our sponsors were now in high gear, and much of their copy got printed—each piece stressing some one item in our equipment or supplies, to the exclusion of everything else. We posed for innumerable photographs, wearing our Snowfire togs, packing tabascomycin in with our medical supplies, checking our Dixon navigation instruments. Farnsworth and Jayne posed together—he looking strong and silent, she slumbrously sultry—for Polar Passion No. 2, the perfume Jayne was to wear at the Pole; the picture didn't tell much about the perfume, but then I suppose it's difficult to photograph a smell. Most of these pix, of course, were unacceptable as editorial matter, but as art-work for ads they found their way into everything from the *New Yorker* to *Iron Age*. Jayne got a nice write-up in one of the exposé magazines, too—and I rather doubt that it exaggerated much; the writer, an anonymous hack who unsigned himself "Harcourt Melish", evidently had been following her career since he was eleven, his tongue hanging out a foot all the way.

In the glare of all this public attention, the Commodore blossomed like a giant hollyhock. The things he said about the expedition became more and more discon-nected from the facts. He told the TV audience on the Garroway show about his dream of finding a hunk of Planet Four-and-a-half, and was delighted to find, next day, that his remarks on that subject had been picked up by the wire services. After that, there was hardly any holding him. Pretty soon he was hinting that he might find virtually the whole protoplanet—or anyhow, half of it—on the floor of the Arctic Ocean, and that the re-covered lump might well show "evidences of life". This, too, was picked up, and front-paged by many of the tabloids, so it wasn't long before the Commodore was speculating in public as to whether or not the proto-planet had been destroyed in an interplanetary war with Mars, and whether or not survivors of the war might have colonized the Earth——

At this point Harriet sat on him so firmly that you

could almost hear the air going out of him. He wouldn't have allowed it if he hadn't enjoyed the process, but obviously he did. But in the nature of things it was impossible to sit on Jayne. Though Harriet stopped Farnsworth's flow of tosh to the press through normal channels, she couldn't prevent Jayne's purveying it in even more highly supercharged form to the Faber chain—after which, of course, it became common coin anyhow.

The reaction was inevitable. A week before the scheduled take off date, I got a telegram from Canada. I had been expecting it. It said:

WHATS GOING ON 2WPBE STOP NEWSPAPER STORIES HERE HIGHLY INACCURATE SENSATIONAL NONSENSICAL STOP IGY COMMITTEE DISTURBED ASKING CLARIFICATION STOP WIRE ME CARE CHUBB CRATER STATION E FREMD

I could hardly blame her. I wired back: COMMODORE DRINKING HEAVY PR WINE AIDED ABETTED SPONSORS PR AGENCIES AND MISS WYNN STOP WILL BE OFF AIR IN WEEK UNTIL THEN WILL TRY SHOOSHING HIM JULIAN COLE

Her reply was short, sharp and pointed:

SHOOSH FIRMLY STOP IGY SPONSORSHIP VERGING WITHDRAWAL E FREMD

After some long and difficult pondering I took all the telegrams—the copy of mine included—to Farnsworth and shoved them at him, without saying a word. He began to bluster almost at once, but the last wire stopped him in mid-eruption.

"Does she mean it?" he said, peering at me sharply. "Surely she's bluffing?"

"Ellen doesn't know the meaning of the word. She

never dealt with anybody in her life on any basis but that of the straight goods." I had this from Ham, of course, not from personal experience; but Ham is a reliable observer. "In some respects it's made her very unhappy, but that's how she is. She says exactly what she means."

"Um." The Commodore chewed at his lower lip. "That's a strange way to deal with people, I must say. But. . . . What do you think I ought to do?"

"Just lay off a little, Geoffrey. Don't let the papers trap you into thinking that everything that gets into print is good for us. If you said tomorrow that you were throwing up the expedition because you'd fallen in love with the Ranee of Krajputni, you'd be on page one of every paper in town—but that kind of publicity isn't worth having. If you can just drop the Space Cadet angle for one more week—and persuade Jayne to drop it, too—we'll be on our way, and the IGY won't be able to yank the rug out from under us. Can't you do that?"

"Uh, yes, I guess I can," Farnsworth said, somewhat mollified, but rather gloomy too. "Nobody in this country has any sympathy with creative imagination any more. It isn't as if I said anything impossible. You know, Julian, this is another piece of the pattern. We've been harassed and bedevilled from the moment we conceived of this expedition. There's no longer any question in my mind about it. *Somebody* doesn't want us to get to the Pole."

"Meaning Ellen Fremd?" I said acidly, against my better judgment. "Horsefeathers, Geoffrey."

"No, not Ellen Fremd directly. But she's being used. It all adds up. She's another piece in the jigsaw puzzle."

"Jigsaw puzzles are pictures that have been cut apart in patterns that have no relationship to the original," I said frostily. "As a model for logic they lead straight to the strait-jacket. Any man who tried to 'use' Ellen Fremd would wind up with blackened stumps where his hands used to be."

"You may be right," he said, in the tone of a man who knew I was wrong.

"Anyhow, Geoffrey, look here, it's very simple. Just lay off the War Between Mars and the Asteroids from now until take off. That's all I ask."

"All right, Julian."

But he was still brooding when I left. I wouldn't have put any money on the staying power of his agreement.

Somehow, all the same, the appointed hour crept closer. That whole week was hotter than Purgatory; I wonder now how any of us lasted it out. Yet take off time did at last arrive.

Were I writing a novel, I would give you here a touching farewell scene between Midge and the kids and me. Under the actual circumstances, nothing could be more inappropriate—not because there wasn't such a scene, but because when take off time arrived, we didn't take off. Bad weather shut in early that morning: thick fog, coupled with a muggy heat more intense than we had had to suffer earlier. There was no chance at all of our getting off the ground, let alone rising above the weather. The planes were so heavily loaded that the heat-rarified air wouldn't have allowed us to reach flying speed before we hit the end of even the longest of Teterboro's runways.

We sat on the field, swearing, while it got hotter and hotter and thicker and thicker, listening with our minds' ears to the expensive aviation petrol evaporating from the tanks. Farnsworth was in a foul mood, but the dogs were in a fouler; not even Elvers could get near them without being snapped at savagely. The result was that after my final farewells I had to trail ingloriously back to Pelham to the unbelieving and disapproving stares of almost the whole brood; only the baby was glad to see me back, and she only because she was too little to understand that I wasn't supposed to be home at all.

The next day was worse, if such a thing is possible. The newspapers, abruptly recalling last year's fiasco, gave us a good going-over, concentrating particularly on the Commodore. He took it badly. Nobody likes being transformed from a hero into a charlatan overnight, and Farnsworth was less well-equipped to take such a transformation philosophically than almost anyone else I can think of. He blamed Harriet for it, out loud and at length.

Harriet's nerves had been as thoroughly fried by the heat as his had been. Nothing in the world is so hot as a hot day at an airport. She got up off the packing box she was sitting on and took the stunned (and, of course, seated) Commodore by both ears.

"Don't you lay your infant troubles on me, you big piece of cheese," she said shrilly. "Anything I did for you I did for free. When was the last time you paid me? What right have you got to complain about volunteer work? Where the hell is my salary?"

The Commodore freed his ears, stood up, and tried to turn his back. Harriet promptly lifted her skirts and kicked him. "Where's my money?" she shouted. "I haven't had one nickel out of your pockets since you took me on."

"Now, Harriet," he said, turning belatedly. "I'm sorry. I spoke hastily. It isn't really your fault, I know that."

"How nice of you to say so. Where's my money? When are you going to pay me my salary? Answer me that!"

A flashlight bulb winked silently. It should be a good picture, I thought, but the photog will rue the day he missed that kick. It had everything, including legs.

"You'll get your money," Farnsworth said. His voice had turned harsh. Evidently he had seen the bulb go off, and he was none too sure whether or not a picture of the kick existed. After all, his back had been turned. "But not if you make a scene, Harriet. Other people trust me. So can you. You'll have to."

"In a pig's eye," she said. Though her voice was now almost as quiet as his, it would have been evident to anyone who knew Harriet as well as I did that she was already on the borderline of hysterics. "You'll pay me, all right. I'm going to stick to you like a burdock. You won't see the last of me until you've coughed up every nickel."

"You won't like the Pole much," Farnsworth said edgily.

"I'm going there, all the same. I'm going to be on your back for the rest of your life—or until I get my salary."

"There isn't room for you."

"Yes there is. I'll sleep with the dogs if I have to. You don't want me to go? All right, pay me. Or lump me. What'll it be?"

Farnsworth shrugged. "I can't pay you now," he said. "Come along if you like."

Harriet burst into tears of triumph. To my utter astonishment Jayne took it upon herself to comfort her and calm her down. The Commodore removed himself to look at the weather.

And the newspapermen broke for the telephones like stampeding cattle.

Luckily, we got off well before the early-bird editions of the papers could reach Teterboro: just at dawn the next morning. I emerged from phoning my family to find Farnsworth in an almost childishly sunny mood; he had just been told that the temperature had dropped enough to permit his planes to get airborne. He was so pleased that he stopped to pat Chinook, Dr. Elvers' lead Malemute; Chinook promptly bit him, high up on one ham, but he responded with nothing more than a desultory kick. (He didn't miss, though. Chinook was still ki-yi-yi-ing over his injured dignity back in the cargo hold when our plane warmed up and drowned him out.)

Only one reporter—a *Times* man—was on hand to watch us tumbling aboard. I found myself seated next to Dr. Eleanor Wollheim, the expedition's bacteriologist and the only other woman involved. She was a strictly utilitarian type, about as glamorous as a potato-masher, and clearly disapproved of men who kicked dogs, or men who were amused by men who kicked dogs. I strapped myself in, secured my oxygen mask in its rack on the back of the seat before me, and looked out the window.

The engines got louder; the plane was trembling markedly as Farnsworth tested each pod in turn. But I wasn't, for once, totally preoccupied with my clammy palms and last-minute urgency to be on the way. Instead I was watching someone running: a wildly

71

gesticulating man, pounding across the field toward us from the direction of the administration building, flourishing what looked to be a roll of blue paper.

Never in my life have I seen anyone so easily identifiable as a process-server. I knew it in the first three seconds after I saw him. Harriet settled down belatedly in the seat immediately in front of me and began to buckle her safety belt. I leaned forward and bellowed in her ear:

"Harriet! Did Farnsworth ever pay Robert Willey, either?"

She looked startledly over her shoulder at me, and then frowned for a moment over my question.

"No," she said.

At the same instant, the plane's engines hit max RPMs, the dogs howled balefully amid the baggage, and Farnsworth let go of the brakes. I was slugged back into my seat, and the gesticulating man vanished instantly. The plane roared down the runway into the lightening mist, noisy, confident, and tail-heavy. As the end of the runway came at us, Farnsworth screwed the flaps down and we went clumsily into the air in one immense bound.

The Second Western Polar Basin Expedition was on its way.

VI

Timid though I am, I have always loved flying, and we had no sooner broken through the cloud-cover than I forgot all the imbroglios of the past months. That flight still sticks in my mind as one of the most beautiful things that has ever happened to me. We emerged over a vast, still sea of clouds flooded with dawn-pink, rolling all the way north to the horizon; after a while I got out of my belt and went forward to watch from the control cabin— a privilege sternly denied passengers on a commercial airliner.

Farnsworth was still piloting, though he could have put the ship on autopilot much earlier had he wanted to. It was evident from his expression that he simply liked flying a plane, and would take a long time further to become bored enough to relinquish manual control. Dr. Hanchett, one of the astronomers, was doing the navigating; he was of course qualified for it, but I rather doubted that he was also properly licensed. Farnsworth was gloriously negligent about little legal details like that; still, who could catch Hanchett operating without a license up here? He was just saving Farnsworth the trouble.

When the cloud-cover finally thinned and vanished, a little over an hour later, we were over Canada by a hair, and forests were rolling away under us. Our air speed was pushing 275, which is good cruising for a B-29; we seemed to be quartering into a strong southeasterly wind. The Commodore was holding us straight-and-level at 13,000 feet—whether zeroed at sea level or at Teterboro I couldn't tell, but it could hardly have made more than 50 feet of difference, not enough to throw off a contact landing for a plane that size. Behind us and to the left was our other plane, cruising just below 10,000—the maximum height at which it's safe to fly without masks in an unpressurized plane.

Farnsworth shot a glance at me and caught me looking at the altimeter. "We'll have to begin climbing for it to-morrow," he said. "There are mountains all along the D. E. W. line here in the east—not as high as the Baffin range, but plenty high enough for these crates."

The plane dipped one wing and he corrected for it, watching the horizon contentedly. I could hardly believe that he was the same man. He seemed almost gentle. All the flamboyance and boisterousness was gone: he was quiet, preoccupied, intense, and yet without a trace of complacence—a man going quietly about a business he knew well.

Abashed, I left him alone. Obviously he could do without being distracted by sightseers like me. I was even beginning to become convinced that he might have managed better if he'd been allowed to have the Flying Tail.

Unused to such an access of humility, I went back to my seat prepared for any self-abasement, even if it involved being polite to Dr. Wollheim. The potato-masher, however, was looking rigidly out the window and needed no help from me. So was Harriet, with a kind of frightened resignation; air travel was old stuff to her, of course, but

74

the destination to which she had committed herself this time was obviously beginning to bulk larger and larger to her. I couldn't help her, either. As for Dr. Wentz, our other astronomer, he had produced a fifth of bourbon from his kit and was getting quietly fried. This was perfectly in character—I had yet to see him sober—and it was obvious that he would be happiest left alone. I knew nothing about him, anyhow, except what I had been able to find in Vol. I of *American Men of Science*— which noted, in cryptic abbreviationese, that his honorary doctorate from the University of Lisbon had been revoked, in the same year that he had been granted it. As for Elvers, he was sleeping with the dogs.

I sat down, feeling perfectly and completely useless. The rest of the human staff was flying behind us with Jayne Wynn. I wondered who was actually piloting that plane. Perhaps she was, considering the broad spectrum of talents I already knew her to have. If so, nevertheless, I was glad not to be with her.

We flew all day and well into the evening. Night fell before we crossed the Sixtieth Parallel, but the ground cover was already sparse by the time the last light failed. This far north, only a few dwarf spruces struggled up against the cold, and at the Sixtieth we would cross the "tree-line", that line which not only divides the trees from the snows, but in Canada traditionally divides the Indians from the Eskimos.

The cabin door opened and the Commodore came out, I suppose because there was nothing more to be seen that day, and came down the aisle. He settled in the seat across from mine, looking pleased with himself.

"Who's minding the store?" I asked him.

"Hanchett. We're on autopilot, and he's watching the instruments. If anything goes wrong he'll call me; he knows enough to detect any trouble." He reached into one of his jacket pockets. "Tell me, Julian, have you ever seen anything like this before?"

"This" proved to be a piece of crudely shaped glass, dark green in colour, about as big as my hand. It was roughly crescent-shaped; on one wing of the crescent, on the outside curve, there was a sort of pool or apron of the same glass, circular when looked down upon.

"No," I said hefting it. It weighed perhaps a quarter of a pound. "Doesn't look much like bottle-glass. What is it?"

"It's Darwin glass—australite."

"Sorry, I'm no geologist. What is it supposed to tell me?"

"Darwin glass," the Commodore explained, "is meteoric. It's one member of a whole family of such glasses, called tektites. They've fallen all over the earth, probably long ago—paleolithic man used them as weapon points. See that puddle?" He pointed to the apron on the back of the crescent. "That's where the surface fused in flight, and the glass flowed back to that point because of the wind-pressure."

Now I was beginning to get his drift. He was back on his favourite hobby-horse, the asteroidal protoplanet. "Do you think they're parts of Planet Four-and-a-half?"

"They couldn't be anything else. Whether or not they were in this glass form when they were actually part of the planet is a tough question. It's possible that glass pools formed on the surface while the planet was still hot, if you assume a world about the size of the Earth, as you

76

pretty well have to. You need a planet with a nickel-iron core, surrounded by a mantle of triolite and olivine, with a top coat of silicates—just like us. Otherwise you can't account for the distribution of meteor-types in any systematic way."

"A planet with a glass skin!" I said. "That would be a novelty."

"I didn't say that," the Commodore objected. "I said silicates—which could mean sand, granite and so on. It's my notion that the tektites were originally parts of comets that passed through the outer layers of the sun's atmosphere, and got converted into glass there. I don't see any other way to account for the low gas pressure they show."

"Then that would indicate that they *weren't* once part of the asteroidal planet, wouldn't it? Comets are supposed to be formed independently."

"Unproven," he said. "I think it's a lot likelier that meteors are just the debris of comets, and that they all came out of the asteroid belt originally."

"Then what happened there originally?"

"Probably a collision," Farnsworth said broodingly. "If there were originally two planets in that area, Jupiter would have been shifting their orbits constantly. After all, the accident had four thousand million years to happen in. The very first tektites fell on the Earth no more than fifty million years ago—and the same seems to hold true of all meteorites, of every kind. You never find them in strata older than that. So the accident was recent."

"You make a good case," I told him sincerely.

"I haven't scratched the surface," he said. "The evidence is overwhelming now. Take Ceres, for instance. It

77

was the first planetoid to be discovered, and it's still the biggest one known. It's also the only one that's known to be spherical. Why is that?"

"Why shouldn't it be? Most planetary bodies are."

"Ah, yes, but *no* asteroids are, except Ceres. The sphericity of a planetary body is its sign and seal that it was in on the original formation of the solar system. You can't heat up a large mass of rock sufficiently by a flash process—such as would be involved in a collision between planets—for it to retain its heat long enough to round off before it cools. You need a temperature of more than three thousand degrees absolute to do that. Ergo, Ceres was not involved in the collision and is not a fragment of either of the colliders. It was a moon belonging to one of them."

"Wow," I said. I meant it. The man's imagination was astonishing.

"Well, what else could it have been?" he said. "It's of exactly the proper size to be a moon of a planet the size of Earth. Our own Moon is enormously too big for us— it's more of a sister planet than a true satellite. If all the planets had been doled out moons on an average basis, ours would be just about five hundred miles in diameter —which happens to be the known diameter of Ceres. And by the way, the tektites weren't formed by any flash process either. Their forming temperatures range from fifteen hundred to twenty-five hundred degrees Centigrade."

I hastily handed the winged bit of dark green glass back to him. I was in no position to weigh his argument on its merits, or even to know whether or not the facts he was spouting at me were really accurate (though where his facts were matchable against those I was carrying in my own head, the agreement was very good). Principally I was beginning to see that this protoplanet obsession of Farnsworth's was going to take up even more of his time and effort at the Pole than I had suspected, very probably to the detriment of the jobs he had been assigned to do by the IGY. I couldn't help being intrigued by what he said, but nevertheless the deeper his preoccupation became, the more likely it was that the expedition would be a fiasco from my point of view; indeed, it could well bankrupt me if I came back with nothing to write about that Ellen Fremd considered worth putting on paper. To be sure, she was interested in Farnsworth's protoplanet too, but she'd lose interest in a hurry if it caused the bulk of the IGY programme to go unfulfilled.

"It's a fascinating logical structure," I said. "I wish I could think we'd be likely to find anything to bolster it up. But frankly, Geoffrey, I doubt that very much."

He put his tektite back in his pocket, his expression abruptly moody. "We'll see," he said. He got up and walked back to the control cabin. I was sorry for him, but glad to see him go; I was suddenly, overwhelmingly sleepy.

Sometime during the night we landed, to take on fuel. I remember dimly hearing the distant howling of dogs, to which only a few of our well-fed animals bothered to respond; then the almost equally-distant jammering of a pneumatic hammer. I looked sleepily out my window over the sprawled bones of Dr. Wollheim. I saw a great expanse of flat snow gleaming under brilliant airfield lights, and black figures and muttering trucks moving about, but I had no idea where we were. In a few moments I was back asleep.

When I woke again, we were airborne, and I had joined the Ancient and Honourable Order of Bluenoses without benefit of initiation. We had crossed the Arctic Circle while I slept. I peered out into the blinding morning.

Have you ever thought of the far North as a luxuriantly colourful country? I certainly had not, nor, to be truthful, did it strike me that way at first. Yet even in the first shock of brilliance I was astonished at the deep blue-violet of the sky against the endless expanse of white, and the radiance of gold, like the leaf in an illuminated manuscript, that the sun laid prodigally over both. Then, gradually, I began to notice tones of blue in the snows, and to realize that they were shadows. The land below me was a true desert, mile after mile of gently undulating, wind-fashioned dunes, made of powder-dry snow instead of sand. The shadows were not evident at first not only because of the dazzlement, but because of "fill"—the light reflected into them from the illuminated sides of the dunes.

Fill not only lightens shadows; it colours them—as the *plein-air* French painters had discovered nearly a hundred years ago. As my eyes continued to adapt to the light, I became more and more aware that what I was seeing thousands of feet below me was truly white only at the peaks of the dunes. There was no true whiteness anywhere else. As the contours of the land changed, as the angle from which I was looking changed with the flight of the plane, as the sun continued to rise, each patch of light and shadow took on a new and even more subtle hue: blue-white, grey-white, pink-white, gold-white, ochre-white . . . as though this mixture of all the components of visible light was constantly giving up first one component colour and then another under the heatless regard of the sun.

The plane's intercom crackled. "We're climbing now," Farnsworth's voice said. "Those of you that are new to this country—Harriet, Julian, Wollheim—don't forget your goggles."

Guiltily, I looked away from the window, and found that I was indeed as blind as a bat. I clawed my way by feel through my kit for my snow-goggles, and then looked out the window again through them until I could once more see the snows; only then was I ready to take them off and look inside the plane. It was still as dark as a coal-pit there, but gradually I was able to make out large objects, and then, with painful slowness, smaller details. It was as frightening as coming out from under ether. Nobody who has undergone snow-blindness is likely to forget it.

Then the mountains began to rise before us, rank on serried rank of them, piling up into the sky in motionless waves of ice-covered, jagged crags. Here and there they were pocketed by lakes—lakes frozen solid all the way down to the bottom, many swept clean enough of snow by the winds to show almost black against the crinkled whiteness of the mountain ranges. Some of these were quitted by river-like, crevasse-knotted extensions which wound down through the valleys for a while toward the south-east and then quit, as sharply as if sheared off like cheese: glaciers. But as we got farther north these too

81

disappeared, leaving us a shimmering universe of grandiose peaks.

We were all alone in this tumbled, cruel ice-scape. Evidently the other plane had taken some more circuitous but easier route. The sense of loneliness was almost tangible. Finally, however, the mountains began to fall behind, and Geoffrey was able to lose altitude little by little.

Though the ice continued for a while without a break, it was easy to tell when we crossed the shoreline of the Arctic Ocean, for the whole character of the surface below changed sharply. It looked now as though it had been coated with clear shellac, and then coated again, layer upon layer, age upon age, until the very earth was covered with a network of fine cracks. After a while I saw the reason for the effect: the ice-sheet here was not continuous, but was instead broken into uncountable thousands of blocks and cakes, which were constantly becoming separated from each other and refreezing again. Each of those "cracks" was a pressure-ridge between two cakes. Here and there I began to see little threads of open water, like pieces of creeks that had somehow gotten lost; and occasionally there was quite a sizeable pond.

There were not many such, however, for the ocean here was chopped up into thousands of islands, each one as snow-capped and desolate as the last, though some of them were as large as Connecticut. Even now, in the summer, it looked as though one could have walked from any one to any other, though the ridges would have made it more of a scramble than a walk. Soon the patches of ice-choked water vanished entirely.

"Coming around on Ellesmere," the Commodore's voice said abruptly. "Fasten your belts, all. It's going to be bumpy."

The engines changed their note. They had been cut back, and the carburettor heaters were labouring to keep from icing; or did a B-29 engine operate by injection? I realized that I just didn't know. In any event, we were now obviously on the first leg of a long landing approach. I had just begun to strap myself down when something prompted me to look back at Wentz. The astronomer's eyes were like black holes in his skull, but he was awake and not too hung over to have understood the instruction; he even managed a ghastly sort of grin when he saw me looking at him.

At five thousand feet the engines broke blue wind and Farnsworth put the flaps down. The terrain did not look any different, except that off to the right I could see tiny black dots that might have been a settlement of some kind. It occurred to me belatedly that Hanchett had by-passed having to cross a second mountain range at the south end of Ellesmere by routing us along the west coast of the big island. If so, that collection of black dots was Alert; indeed, we were banking in that direction now.

Despite Farnsworth's warning, the landing was not very bumpy—certainly no more so than the normal airline landing at a small city. Alert was too cold to provide any thermals large enough to bother a B-29. Farnsworth did supply us with a good high bounce when we first touched ground, but he was bold enough to feather the props and roar us into a power stall almost before we touched again. We smacked down promptly and rolled to a stop at the head of a huge white comet.

By that time I was convinced enough of Farnsworth's piloting skill to be a little surprised to see, after the snow had settled, that there were ambulances and fire-trucks boiling toward us from all sides. Nobody was so much as bruised, so we sent them all away again. Some of the crews looked a little disappointed; living inside the Arctic Circle was, apparently, dull most of the time, and they had thought they had a sure thing when they saw Farnsworth belly-whopping on to a field as slippery as oil on asphalt.

I enjoyed sneering at their disappointment. I felt like an old Polar hand already.

I felt like a freeze-dried Brussels sprout ten seconds after I had stepped into that wind for the first time. My parka, goggles and patches—on my cheeks, nose and chin —seemed to make no difference at all. I might as well have been naked. It was 30 below out there. The figure tells you absolutely nothing; either you've felt it, or you haven't. And this, mind you, was spring.

Farnsworth gave us no time to think, had the cold left us any such ambition. We were all hustled into a Quonset at the edge of the field, heaped neatly inside with the supplies which had been cached on the preceding trip. The stove had been fired in advance of our landing; I was propped next to it on one side, to thaw, and Wentz on the other to cook sober; somehow he had managed to get another edge on during the landing run. Then the place was empty, very suddenly. The rest of the crew had gone off either to the operations hut to monitor Jayne's plane in, or to service the snowmobiles in their snow-blanketed hangar.

I was now warm enough to shiver without fear of chipping myself, and I went at it like a man with malaria. Wentz watched me owlishly for a few moments and then produced a bottle from somewhere inside his parka. Theoretically he had been deprived by Farnsworth of the bottle he had been working on, so this one must represent an emergency cache; but the flat pint was already a third empty.

"Have some," he said with childlike directness. "Warm you up."

Bourbon is not my idea of a breakfast juice but I squeezed that bottle manfully before returning it, all the same. After a while I either stopped shivering or stopped noticing it. "Thanks," I said.

"Don' mention it. Good for you. Don' ever do that onna ice, though. Freeze you stiff b'fore you feel it. Happened t' many a man." He took a swig himself, his Adam's apple working up and down. He must have had an oesophagus sheathed in vanadium steel; the raw stuff went down like orange pop.

"Believe me, I won't," I said. The whisky had hit me hard; I was already making glib resolutions for my to-morrow's sober self. Somewhere in the back of my head, however, was second-hand confirmation of Wentz's advice; all the authorities say that it is fatal to drink to warm yourself up while you're in the field. I wondered how a man with his thirst would be able to knock off when we, in turn, were actually out in the weather.

"When do you think Mrs. Farnsworth will get here?"

"Jayne? Inna while. I don't miss her. More damn foolishness with the movies."

"Movies? Are we going to take films?"

"We already took plenty," Wentz said gloomily. "Last

85

time we were up here. Last year, you know, with the snow buggies."

He stretched out both his feet in front of him and looked at them as though he had never seen them before. "Geoffrey hadda cameraman with him then. To take shots at the Pole. Took a lot of 'em right here, just in case we din *get* to the gawdam Pole. We din get there, all right."

"Who's the cameraman? I guess I didn't meet him."

"Oh, he isn't here *now*," Wentz said. "Geoffrey din't pay him. Gave him fifteen hundred on account and his fare back stateside, on a TCA plane. He sued us for his other ten thousand. Got two hundred fifty bucks and glad to get it, that's a cinch. Vanother?"

I hadda nother. "Why did he want so much?"

"Well, Geoffrey offered him that much," Wentz said moodily. "Besides, it was four months out of his life. And my God, the film. Thousands of feet. Jayne puttin' on lipstick witha glacier inna background. Jayne puttin' on lipstick witha snowbuggy inna background. Jayne puttin' on lipstick witha nicefield inna background. Jayne puttin' on lipstick witha gawdam *dogs* inna background. Jayne——"

He was beginning to sound more and more like *Finnegans Wake*. "Who's going to take the films if we really do make the Pole this time?" I cut in hastily.

"Me." Glug, glug.

"Oh." I thought about that for a moment. "Tell me something, Dr. Wentz. Does Farnsworth pay you? He doesn't seem to pay anybody else very regularly."

"Now an' then he pays me," Wentz said. "Thass all right. I'm a lush, you know? No ob-ser-va-tory's goin'

86

to hire *me*. Ol' Geoffrey, he hires me. Pays me sometimes. Now and then, you know? Thass all right. I'm chief of 'stronomy for the whole ex-pe-di-tion, thass who *I* am. An' director of photography for the film, when we show the film. Right there onna title cards. Thass who. Bassar that sued ol' Geoffrey gets a lil line in agate type, says he's cameraman's assistant. Show *him*, you know? Secon' Wessern Polar Bassar Ex-pe-di-tion, thass who. Le's havva drink."

But the bottle continued to hang there from his hand, its bottom nearly touching the splintery floorboards. He went on watching his shoes, as though he were afraid they might get him up and take him somewhere. When, cautiously, I peered more closely at him, I saw that he was out with his eyes open.

And I was alone. An impenetrable barrier of alcohol and frustration between me and the nearest human being; an expedition full of madmen between me and sanity; hundreds of miles of ice and wilderness between me and the rest of the world; hundreds of hours of desolation between me and the future . . . and north of me a rock slumbered—I could almost believe it now—millions of miles from the planet that gave it birth, with the very bones of Creation frozen at its core. . . .

A plane passed low overhead, but I hardly heard it. For the first time, now that I was all by myself, I was listening to the wind.

Book Two

VII

The incoming plane had been Jayne. She and her party had almost frozen solid, despite their furs and masks, during the last half of their flight in their unpressurized craft; the biting winds on the airfield must have seemed almost mild to them. Luckily there were no frostbites. They came trooping into the thawing shack, where they made a great to-do flapping their arms about, stamping and blowing on their fingers. None of this noise disturbed Dr. Wentz in the least; he sat slumped where he was, seventy per cent unfrocked astronomer and thirty per cent bourbon ("This whisky guaranteed to be at least three months old—Coloured and flavoured with wood chips").

"That's enough," Jayne said at last. "Let's get this show on the road. Coming, Julian?"

She did not seem in the least tired, though the flight must have been gruelling. I shrugged and got up. I didn't relish the notion of going out into that cold again, but at least the trip would be short—and I was glad to have conscious company once more, even if it had to be Jayne. Some of the other members of her group were not so willing:

"Hey, have a heart, Miss Wynn."

"Can't we wait another five or ten minutes, at least? I'm still blue right down to my boots."

"It's warm in the operations hut," Jayne said. "I've

got to get a release on the air in time for the bulldog editions, and there's no radio in this damn hole. Let's move."

They grumbled, but they climbed back into their togs. "What about him?" Fred Klein said.

Jayne barely bothered to glance at Wentz. "He's as useful here as he'd be over there," she said scornfully. "Let him alone."

"Well, but let's at least pass the bottle," Sidney Goldstein suggested. Nobody waited for Jayne to okay this idea; the bottle was plucked at once from Wentz's dangling hand. By the time it got to me it was empty, but I'd already had my share. Then we ploughed out into that blinding cold again.

The operations hut was already crowded when we got there, and after that it was close to impassable. I counted noses with difficulty and found that everyone was there but Elvers (and, of course, Wentz). Evidently Farnsworth had conned help from the enlisted men of the base complement for the job of finishing servicing the snowmobiles. Maybe Elvers was supervising. The base commandant, Col. McKinley, was also there, with two aides; all three of them watched us mill around with expressions that varied between amusement and alarm. I could understand how they felt; there was something about the gathering that resembled children just arrived at a party which was on the verge of being too large to control.

Jayne unpacked her typewriter and got right to work on top of a foot-locker. She had a preposterous release about our landing and our further preparations all written in about ten minutes. She showed it proudly to both Harriet and me.

"You can't send that," I protested. "For one thing, it's a phony."

"Julian, your tune never changes," she said. I think she was genuinely hurt. "It isn't a phony. It's *essentially* true. Of course we haven't done all of these things yet, but we're going to. And how often am I going to find time to radio home, once we're really working?"

"Twice a day?" Harriet suggested. Her smile was scared, but she was trying.

"The deskmen back home will smell it out," I insisted. "If they don't, the technically informed people will—including the IGY Committee."

She sniffed. I had a good idea what I could do with my IGY Committee. Nor could I sway her an inch; Harriet, wisely, didn't even try. In the end the release went out just as she had written it. I could only hope that the papers would have sense enough to tone it down—except for the Faber chain, which of course would print it verbatim. But if the *Times*, for instance, printed it with some of those cosy bracketed interpolations of theirs, the wire services would get the interpolations moving as short "adds" to the main story, and even the Faber chain might print those. After all, Jayne was their girl, and any news about the expedition, even if it corrected her copy, would in a sense be news about her. . . .

I was already getting to be expert at whistling past graveyards.

The door opened, letting in a banshee scream of wind and finely powdered snow, and Elvers' face peered at us from under his parka. Everybody yelled at him and he shut himself out at once.

Farnsworth had jostled his way over to the commandant's desk, where he spread his charts out and bent over them, frowning, his big forefinger stabbing here and there for Hanchett's benefit. "It's not going to be as simple as it looks," he was saying. "I'd be happier if there were a few small islands north of us to anchor the ice and give us base points. As it is, there's just no place to drive a bench-mark once we leave Ellesmere."

"We can't cross over the Otterloo Current in any case with the machines," Hanchett said. "It'd be better to follow a curve off to the west, even if it does take us farther from the mainland."

"You're going to try to go all the way to the Pole in those moving-vans of yours?" Col. McKinley said incredulously.

"That's why we brought them up here."

"You can't do it," the commandant said. "Those vehicles are totally unsuitable for summer work on the ice. The cap isn't continuous in the summer—it's just pack ice. You can't put that much weight on it."

"We'll manage," Farnsworth said. "That's what we've got experts with us for."

"No such thing as an expert up here. The Arctic Ocean is the least explored area in the whole world. That damned ice is untrustworthy in the summer, and that's that. You'll never make it in those machines."

Farnsworth straightened, his face darkening. I realized that I had never seen him really angry before. "Look here, Colonel," he said evenly. "I'm the man who's running this expedition. I'm being paid to run it, by some of the biggest businesses in the world; they think I know what I'm doing. So do I."

"I don't," Col. McKinley said, staring back at Farnsworth with an expression as sardonically motionless as an Easter Island statue. "I've been up here two years, and I'm not an expert. You got here today. Draw the moral."

"I have no time for that kind of exercise, nor any patience with it. If I leave my snowbuggies behind, I lose my trade-mark, which is worth many thousands of dollars. I also fail to fulfill my testing commitments to my sponsors. I also lose most of my ability to be of use to the government, and to the International Geophysical Year. Therefore, the buggies go, and with your co-operation. This is what I say. That makes it so."

Col. McKinley stood stock still for a moment; then he spread his hands and shrugged. "Those are the orders I have," he said harshly. "Hell, Commodore, I'm not trying to run your expedition. I'm just trying to keep you from committing suicide. Go ahead, do it your way; it's no skin off my nose."

Farnsworth smiled winningly. "Thank you, sir," he said. "I don't want to be bull-headed either. I'll go along with you this far: Suppose I take one of our planes over the proposed route, first? If there are serious conditions anywhere along the path, Hanchett and I can easily plot a new course around them. That ought to keep us out of trouble."

"It'll get you shot down, too," McKinley said, with a certain relish. "I'm sorry, Commodore, but that's out of the question. I am empowered to forbid that kind of operation, and I do forbid it."

"Why, in God's name?" Farnsworth said, his face changing colour again.

"Because this is a military area—or a theatre of war, if you really want the blunt name for it. For an IGY outfit, you people seem to be pretty light on facts the IGY knows by heart. Were you at the Stockholm IGY meeting in 1956?"

"No," Farnsworth said. "What has that to do with it?"

"The Russians proposed then that we and they fly alternate daily observation patrols across the Pole, landing at each other's bases at Nome and Murmansk. Our people weren't empowered to accept, but later on Washington accepted, with conditions. The Russians accepted the conditions."

"Well?"

"One of the conditions rules out all unscheduled flights. Only normal commercial traffic and the agreed transpolar patrol are allowed. The violating party is liable to attack on sight. There are fighters up all the time to enforce the rule—we've even had a few inconclusive dogfights, and one of those could blow up into something major any time now. If you take one of those crates of yours over the Pole, the Russians will shoot you down, and we'll just have to sit back and watch them do it. If we stepped in, in violation of the agreement, we'd start a war—after all, we made the conditions ourselves. Clear enough?"

"Perfectly," Farnsworth said, unruffled. "All right, no planes. We'll just have to do it the hard way—in the snowmobiles. Very good. Jayne, come over here and let's check the crews."

McKinley was shunted aside, wearing the expression of a man who has won all the battles and lost the war. The manœuvre was purely dramatic on Farnsworth's part, for there was not a great deal of planning left to do. The lead snowbuggy would be driven by Dr. Hanchett,

93

who had the responsibility of seeing to it that we would follow the proposed path into the interior, and arrive on time at the Pole instead of somewhere on the north coast of Greenland. As the next most valuable members of the party, Elvers and the dogs would ride in the last buggy, which Jayne would drive, because only a total of four people in the party knew how to drive them. This meant that Harriet had to ride in the middle buggy with Farnsworth because she would not be separated from her paycheque, so I decided to ride in the middle buggy too, along with Sidney Goldstein, our cheerful cryologist, who professed to be much smitten with Harriet. Wentz was put in with Jayne and Elvers on the theory that he would be in no shape to care whom he rode with, though it wasn't expressed quite that openly. Wollheim was to go with Hanchett in order to make sure that there was one woman in each buggy, thus dividing the risk to what little of potential American motherhood we had with us.

And so on. It was all very sane and unexcited, like parcelling out passengers for a three-car picnic. All through the allocation the wind howled without let or surcease, and somewhere along the line I found Harriet's hand curled in mine, like a hedgehog warming its nose in its burrow.

We got up at 5.00 a.m. the next day, but it was nearly noon outside, as it had been for many weeks. I was getting my first taste of what it is like to live in a country where the days and nights are each six months long, and the sun goes down a little and then rises again in the sky without ever having set. Above the Acrtic Circle, Kepler

94

and God are superseded by something called Benchley's Law, which says that the Earth does not really go around the Sun at all, but around Aroostook, Me., and besides there is really no such place anyhow.

When there is no Time, you make one up; and man-made time is always fast. At least in the beginning, I would have eaten five or six meals a day, slept twice as often as usual, and wound up the week on only three or four clock-days, had it not been for clocks and the wise condescension of old Arctic hands among the young draftees on the base. My metabolism was enormously speeded up, by the cold perhaps, and, I think, by my drive to get through the calendar months and back home. Without clocks, I would have aged several years in those two months, out of inability to recognize when a given astronomical day actually was over.

By the time I arrived in the cave where the snow-mobiles were stored, it was already deafening with the echoes of two of their engines. Mechanics were heating the block of the third engine with a huge blowtorch, and before long it too was slamming noise off the walls. In the darkness after the snow-glare, the buggies looked like crouching animals, their gigantic tyres—almost as high as they were—tucked under their blunt chins like paws.

Inside, however, they were warm and comfortable, and surprisingly roomy. If you take a vehicle almost as big as a two-story house, and apportion the space inside it as economically as you would apportion it in a submarine, you can pack in a lot of living space along with the necessary equipment, and Farnsworth's designer hadn't stinted. The impression of being on shipboard was heightened in the tiny driver's cab, which was laid out like a miniature ship's bridge.

Farnsworth was up there when I came in, humming something repetitious and full of flatted fifths which I suppose was African, and watching the elaborate dashboard while the engine warmed up.

"Hello, Julian," he said abstractedly. "Find your cabin all right? Enough room? Got your things stowed away?"

I gave him a blanket yes and watched over his shoulder. The doors to the cave were being swung open now, letting in the intense white glare and lighting up the hunched shoulders of Hanchett's snowmobile ahead of us. Abruptly the basketwork dish atop Hanchett's machine began to revolve on its alt-azimuth mounting. The astronomer was testing his radar, the invisible lifeline he would use to keep us together across the ice.

"Geoffrey, this is Number One," his voice squawked abruptly from the radio imbedded in the dash. "Do you read me?"

"Loud and clear," Farnsworth said into his hand mike.

"Jayne, come in. Do you read me?"

"Loud and clear, Number One."

"Number Two to Number One," Farnsworth said. "Let's check out on the engines."

"I'm missing Wentz here," Jayne said. "Hold it—they tell me he's here. Evidently he slept here. All right, Geoffrey, call 'em off."

They were as formal as airline pilots in calling in their oil temperature, magneto readings, and twenty other details, but I was in no doubt that the instrumental ballet was necessary. It reassured me, a little. At last Farnsworth said: "All right, Number One, it's your lead."

There was a moment's pause through which the three snowmobile engines snarled *sotto voce*. Then Dr. Hanchett sounded his air-horn—a ferocious, inanimate bugling which made my scalp tighten—and his snow-buggy hunched down and rolled out into the intolerable day. Farnsworth shifted gears, our own engine roared, and I felt us begin to move out after him.

"Here we go," Farnsworth said detachedly. "You look a little nervous, Julian. Did you sleep poorly?"

"I was awake a good deal," I admitted. "The wind was noisy."

"Tcha. Here." He produced a small round pillbox of transparent plastic, rather like a glass model of a young oyster, from his pocket and handed it to me. It was full of little orange tablets.

"What are these?"

"Tranquizol, ten milligrams. Something Pfistner makes; good for the nerves."

The hell with that; I handed it back to him. I had successfully resisted the antihistamine craze in the old days when they were being boomed as cures for colds, and I meant to go right on resisting them now that they were being called ataraxics. I don't exactly enjoy my anxieties, but they are my personal property and I mean to keep them.

"I'm not tense, just tired. And I want to keep alert so I can report accurately. That's why I'm here."

"Very good." He tossed one of the orange pills into his mouth without seeming to notice that he had done it, and stowed the box away. Ahead, Hanchett's machine

97

crossed the boundaries of the airfield and began to wind north among the heaped drifts. Farnsworth followed him closely.

"It's a great adventure, Julian," he said. "We're coming closer every minute to one of the greatest riddles in creation. I know we are. If we could actually solve it. . . ."

"I admire your faith. You've even almost convinced me—and I'm a hard man to convince."

"Want more facts? Julian, I have them by the thousands. You shushed me when I told the newspapers that we might find evidences of life in any protoplanet fragments we brought up. Did you know then that somebody already has?"

"I didn't know it," I said, "and as a matter of fact I don't believe it."

"But it's true. Bacteria were cultured from the interiors of meteorites, more than twenty years ago."

"Oh, that. I remember those experiments. They were pretty well discredited. The sterile techniques the experimenters used weren't foolproof by any means, as I remember it. And the germs themselves turned out to be pretty commonplace—*Bacillus subtilis*, and some other almost universal Earth types."

"But what do you want a meteoric bacterium to do—sing 'Stars Fell on Alabama', or show hotel stickers from Jupiter on its luggage?" Farnsworth demanded. "I'd like to meet the taxonomist today who'd offer me money that those microbes were one hundred per cent identical with *subtilis*. Doctor Wollheim once told me that she wouldn't certify the ancestry of any bacterial cell without a phage typing, and even then she still wouldn't be sure of its orthoclone, whatever that is. What did they know about bacterial genetics in those days?"

"So the experiment was inconclusive; sure. That's all I'm saying. Ergo, it has no standing as evidence."

Farnsworth sighed. "You're indeed a hard man to convince, Julian. Maybe I'd best leave you alone and let you convince yourself. When *I* try to convince you, you feel obliged to fight back."

It was, I realized, a disturbingly accurate capsule analysis of how I think. Obviously Farnsworth was not yet done with surprising me.

I never knew when we passed over the shoreline of Ellesmere and went out over the ocean itself. The pressure ridges in the ice along the shoreline extended more than a mile inland, and nearly that far north, too, so that our progress through them was long. It was not, however, monotonous, for these ridges are comparatively long-lasting, and so are sculptured by the wind into sharp, interconnected statues and curious shapes full of oval holes, every one opalescent with captured sunlight. It was like moving through an ocean made, not of water, but of transparent driftwood.

By the time we were facing the serrated ice-field that rolled without visible break over the horizon to the Pole, there was no land under us at all—nor had there been any for several hours.

Here we were able to pick up speed. Hanchett's snowmobile accelerated cautiously until he was doing about twenty miles an hour, with occasional delays as he spotted some ridge or dip that might mean trouble. Alone, he might have been able to go even faster; but in any train of vehicles there is a whip-crack effect as the last car in line tries to keep up; since the driver of the last car never decides where it is that he's going, he loses two or three seconds of decision-time on every minor turn, and the only answer to that is speed. The result is that if the head car is doing a steady fifty, the rear car may well be doing ninety at least half of the time—and one of these days we are going to lose a President to just this effect of a motorcade.

Hanchett's machine, with its eternally revolving radar antenna, was the only thing to look at in the whole snowbound world now. What he could be using to relieve his eyes and keep his sense of perspective I could hardly imagine. Now and then he spoke to us, but always only on business. There was considerable chit-chat back and forth by radio between Jayne's buggy and ours, which Hanchett must have heard—since the channel was always open—but he never contributed to any of the purely social talk; the strain must have been tremendous.

How Farnsworth had managed to get two such dif-ferent men as Hanchett and Wentz as his astronomers could not be riddled. I kept thinking, with irritation at the irrelevance of the pun, that they were poles apart.

The sky was clear all day, without a trace of snow. A little spume blew off the surface of the ice, but the snow there was too hard-packed to impede visibility much. At noon I went below to eat, and found even Harriet less pale. Our progress had been so smooth that her ready fears were beginning to submerge, and she was parrying Sidney Goldstein's deliberately outrageous flirting with almost the old Madison Avenue gusto. By the time the three of us left the galley together for the bridge, we were quite cheerful; Farnsworth was as pleased with us as a father.

"No news," he told us, attacking the corned beef sandwich we had brought him with the tilting of the head and the sudden *snap* of a striking turtle. "Mm. I was hun'ry. Parm me."

We settled into crannies and peered out the broad windshield. Farnsworth did for his sandwich in about five bites and drank all his coffee. "I saw one of the patrol planes Colonel McKinley was talking about back at the airfield. An F-one-o-one. Elvers says his dogs are all thriving, and that's good for huskies. Ordinarily they get carsick within the first hour. Harriet, my dear, are you still angry with me? You look beautiful. I think you're beginning to enjoy yourself."

"I'm not angry," Harriet said. "I'm glad I came along, I'll admit it. I just wish I believed you're going to pay me when this is all over, Geoffrey."

"I swear I will. Believe me, Harriet; I give you my oath." He looked at her with great earnestness for a moment, and then turned back to his driving. Harriet glanced at me. I tried to convey that I thought Farnsworth meant it, though I was still reserving judgment despite my growing admiration for the man; but there are limits to what one can convey with a shrug and a half-nod and a one-quarter smile which tilts in the wrong direction. Harriet resumed looking through the windshield, the hard violet glare throwing shadows into her eye-sockets and under her cheekbones. The effect was rather like what happens to women's faces under fluorescent lighting, but without the tinge of sallowness; by God, it *did* make her look beautiful.

"Number One to Number Two. Geoffrey, we're pulling up. There's a long fissure dead ahead. It's very heavily faulted. I think we'd better have a sounding; is Sidney available?"

"Right here," the cryologist called toward Farnsworth's mike. "Available Goldstein, at your service."

Farnsworth backed the snowmobile down into low-low gear and then braked it gingerly. Hanchett's snow-buggy was immobile about fifty yards ahead of us, its radar dish going round and round with idiot conscientiousness. I peered through the periscope and saw Jayne's machine panting into view behind us.

"Do you want to set off a charge here, Sid?" Farnsworth said. "There's no reason why we shouldn't start taking soundings now, as far as I can see."

"I want to look at that fault, first. I don't want to risk making it worse; this is a tidal zone. If I think it can stand it, why not? That's what we brought the dynamite for." He left to get into his parka.

Some ten minutes later, we saw him trudging away across the ice with his kit, absurdly foreshortened, towards Hanchett's vehicle, where he stopped and just stood for a while. Then he disappeared into the lead buggy.

We waited, listening to the snoring of our idling engine, while the high thin stillness of the top of the world piled in invisible drifts around us.

"Number One to Number Two. Sidney votes against firing any charge here. We'll go ahead about half a mile and stop there for a test boring. Better sit tight until you pick up the concussion, or we report that there isn't going to be one."

"Right. Does it look serious?"

"Sidney says no. Maybe I'm being overcautious. But I think we ought to test, before we cross on to what may be thinner ice."

"Right." Farnsworth touched a button, and there was a small muffled explosion underneath us: a shotgun charge, driving a piton into the ice. The piton would act as a sonar probe to pick up the sound of Sidney's explosion; the echo should offer a good index of the thickness of the ice at the point of detonation.

"Jayne, are you set for Sid's echo?"

"All set."

Hanchett's snowmobile began to crawl forward, almost imperceptibly. Its nose went up and then down, and then one rear wheel lifted high on its independent suspension, as though the squat square animal had mistaken one of the ice-sculptures for a fireplug. Then the vehicle was climbing up again, out of the fissure. On the other side, Hanchett halted for a moment, and then resumed creeping.

"All clear," Hanchett's calm voice reported.

I was having difficulty in keeping the perspectives straight at this distance. Hanchett's buggy seemed to be much harder to see than it should be, at the snail's pace at which it was moving. Furthermore, it seemed to be dwindling in reverse perspective, the whiteness rising around its bottom, as though the horizon were intervening behind him and us. I looked at Farnsworth; he was frowning, obviously as baffled as I was.

The snowmobile stopped again. Nevertheless, it continued to become more difficult to see. The sky was as clear as ever.

"What the hell?" Farnsworth said plaintively. "Doc, are you moving?"

"No," the radio said. "We've developed a slight list. Hold on; we're checking."

The white horizon between us and the buggy rose again, with a marked jerk. Now I could see the list. Hanchett's snowmobile was tilted slightly to the right, and it was slewed that way a little, too. So was the impossible intervening horizon.

The fault was sliding. I tried to shout and found my throat filled with glue. Farnsworth had seen it, however. He hit the transfer-case on our buggy into middle-low gear and we lurched forward, our wheels spinning and slipping despite their four-point drive.

"Grapnels!" he bawled. "Lines! Everybody into suits! Jayne, get under way!"

I turned to beat it down below, but he caught me by the wrist. "Not you," he said. "I need you." The buggy lurched into high-low.

By the time we reached the edge of the fissure, it had tipped entirely free of the pack. Hanchett's machine rested with absurd solemnity on the tilting floe for long seconds, like a fly on a wall.

"Hanchett! Back up, in God's name!"

Hanchett's rear wheels began to turn backwards, slowly. His machine slid downhill, turning in a slow circle. The ice-ridge on our left screamed, broke free and reared skyward. Hanchett coolly turned his front wheels in the direction of the skid, but he had no traction now. The buggy went down the flat slope like a runaway roller-skate.

It struck the black water on the other side at right

angles and fell over. The radio rang like a gong. The ice-cake, freed of the car's weight, caught it by the wheels on the other side and turned it over on its back, mangling it like a chunk of taffy. Someone cried out—I shall never know who, for the sound came out of our radio in a great blare of unfocused despair, impossible to identify.

Then the snowbuggy dropped straight down into the Arctic Ocean and was gone. There was a great blurt of an air-bubble as it vanished, flinging up spray that went floating away as ice-crystals on the wind. The ice-floe heeled back toward us, heeled again, rocked back, groaned, and was peremptorily frozen into place in the white world again, slightly out of true.

There was nothing left but ice, and a peculiar mechanical sound which I identified first, quite crazily, with the peeping of Hanchett's guide-beam as he sank. After I identified the sound properly, I felt crazier than ever, for it was not mechanical at all. It was a human voice, coming from the cab in the buggy behind us.

Hip-ip-ip-ip! Hip-ip-ip! Hip-ip! Hip-ip-ip-ip-ip! Hip-ip-ip!

Farnsworth took his microphone by the throat, his face savage, but words had failed him at last. To the north another, smaller plume of spray went up: above the spot where Hanchett was still plunging toward the bottom of the Arctic Ocean, there was now a blow-hole in the ice-cap.

And Elvers was giggling. I will remember that sound as long as I live.

VIII

We had to stop there. Hanchett had been our only sober astronomer, and our only navigator. We had also lost Dr. Wollheim, and Dr. Benz, our senior oceanographer, and Ben Taurasi, our engineer-mechanic. We had been crazy to put Hanchett and Taurasi in the lead buggy, but it was too late to know better now. They were gone. So were Sidney Goldstein and Benz, on both of whom we had been planning to depend for survival on this frozen ocean.

And Wollheim was gone too. She wanted to live no less, however we had valued her. In this white desert any life was precious, as it is precious anywhere, even in the deserts of cities. I had never known that before, but I knew it now, and it scared the hell out of me. It still does. I keep thinking that people I despise have as much right to life as I do, and it's not a thought that I like. But when I see now in my unforgiving memory the black bubble that was the end of Dr. Wollheim, I remember that I was pleased to see her go—after all, she was unpleasant to look at, and no good to me—and I am terrified still at my own cruelty and indifference. Forgive me, poor bag of bones. I need your forgiveness; you no longer need anything.

That is what I ask for now, but it was not my first reaction. When I was small, I lived in my grandparents' house with my mother, who was divorced and was doing very badly at supporting us by teaching singing. I had very little consciousness of the struggle, or of the bitterness that underlay it in the household on both sides, until the day that I broke my glasses in some scramble or other—I forget just what.

It was a quiet summer afternoon when I came back to the house; I found my mother sitting in her second-floor room at her vanity-table, one of the few pieces of furniture that she had not sold after the divorce. I told her what had happened, and tendered the pieces—one lens and the frame still intact, and every scrap of the broken lens, for I knew even then that opticians could get measurements from the pieces to make a new lens. I felt rather proud of myself for having salvaged it all.

To my astonishment and fright, she burst into tears; and what she said was, "How am I ever going to pay for it now?"

I ran to my own room and shut the door. I puzzled painfully about it all the rest of the day, and finally emerged with the only solution I could see: a cache of a dollar and seventy-two cents I had been putting together all summer long out of my allowance. My mother had stopped crying by that time, but she took the money without comment, leaving me feeling as though nothing whatever had been settled. It would never have occurred to me then that she had not been crying about the money at all, but about the disability—for it had never seemed like much of a disability to me. Indeed, I didn't make the connection until years later, when I remembered that she had also cried the day I had the glasses put on me for the first time.

This is something that the Greeks never knew about

tragedy, for it is an exclusive discovery of the twentieth century: that first reactions to tragedy are almost invariably wildly trivial and inappropriate, because the deep emotions that they call forth drag with them associations from the still-living past which seem more real, because they have been lived with longer, than the immediate event itself seems. It would never have occurred to even so mighty an artist as Sophocles, for instance, to have put into my mind, at the moment I saw the snowbuggy disappear, this first desperate cry: *But it isn't MY fault at all!*

But then, nobody has ever accused Sophocles of having been near-sighted.

Farnsworth, too, was shaken; God alone knew what *his* first reactions could have been. He said very little, but he promptly gave up any vestige of his desire to take the snowbuggies to the Pole that might have remained after the disaster. Jayne recovered first, at least enough to remind him tentatively of the commercial stake we had in using the snowbuggies. He snarled her down in four short, raw, ugly words, seemingly printable enough in themselves, but delivered to Jayne in a voice I would not use to a garbage-robbing tramp. It stunned everyone; there was a long silence. It was as though he had relieved himself at the foot of a monument.

"Shut up," was what he said. "Make camp."

Those were the four words; no more than that. And that is what they sounded like.

We made camp with a minimum of talk, tying down the remaining buggies, setting up our fifty-foot radio mast and our wind generator, and taking intensive inventory of what we had lost in the way of equipment in the lead buggy. It was hard work getting the mast up, even with the winch, and I for one raised a good sweat inside my outdoor clothes. Nevertheless, I was astonished to see Elvers industriously cutting fifty-pound blocks of ice, wearing nothing but cleated shoes, wool socks, shorts and a jacket. I pointed him out to Farnsworth while we rested from hauling on a guywire.

"What does he think he's doing? He must be out of his mind."

"He's odd," Farnsworth said grimly. "But he's working. He's going to build an igloo for the dogs. They're supposed to live outdoors whenever possible."

"No, I mean running around half naked like that."

"I notice you're sweating, Julian. There's almost no wind, so he isn't likely to get frostbitten. He knows the North. Right now he's in more danger from sunburn than he is from the cold. See if you can snub that loop around the peg on the next heave."

We met that "evening", after a dinner which nobody ate much of, in the galley in Farnsworth's buggy. We were a markedly gloomy and depleted group, especially since neither Elvers nor Harry Chain was there; Elvers was still working, and Harry was testing the radio. None of those present seemed to want to look any of the others in the face for longer than a few seconds at a time, and I noticed that Wentz, who had been shocked sober and had remained that way all the rest of the day, working with the rest of us, for once did not look any more haggard than anybody else.

"It comes down to this," Farnsworth said at last, in oddly muffled tones. "We're going to leave the buggies here as a home base, and make the Pole our advance base. We'll go on by sled, taking only what we need. At the Pole we'll set up the tents, but we'll also build igloos for the research projects to operate in. You've all been watching Elvers and you can see that there's no trick to it, beyond having sufficient structural visualization to trim the blocks right. If you get into trouble, Elvers will be available to help you. He'll drive the lead team, with Jayne; I'll bring up the rear with Fred Klein, and Wentz will be in the middle with Julian. Harriet, you and Harry Chain will stay here; in an emergency, you'll have Harry to drive the buggy."

He looked from one to another of us, sombrely. "This isn't how we planned it, but it's how it's going to have to be," he said. "Harriet, I know you're determined to stick to me until you get your cheque. But this time you're going to have to give in. You're totally ignorant of any skill we can use at the advance base. Here at the home base you just might save all the rest of our lives. Understand?"

"No, not entirely," Harriet said. I noticed, however, that her voice was quiet and steady. "What good am I here, for that matter?"

"You're a lifeline," Farnsworth said. "Harry's a healthy young man, but he still has the appendix God gave him when he was born. If he were here all alone, and it should act up——"

"I see. Harry will teach me to run his radio, just in case. All right, Geoffrey. I'm scared, but I'll do as you say."

I was proud of her, and, I think, so was Farnsworth, in some way I couldn't understand.

Wentz put up his hand.

"Yes, Joe, what is it?"

"Geoffrey," the astronomer said, "have you given any thought to turning back? Fun is fun, but I'm beginning to wonder if I see the joke any longer. With a third of our personnel and equipment gone, we're in trouble right where we sit—and we could make it back to Alert in maybe six hours, if we don't hit any more trouble."

"That needed to be said, and I'm glad you said it," Farnsworth agreed. "I'll say this: Jayne and I are not going back. I'd be sorry to lose you, Joe, but you can go back if you like. Anybody who wants to leave can get in the other snowmobile; we'll make do with one."

"No, no. You're making a melodrama out of it," Wentz said. "I'm not proposing a mutiny or a mass desertion, and it isn't fair to turn it into an appeal for loyalty. All I wanted to know was whether you'd thought about turning back. It's a serious question. There's no room in it for challenges or heroics."

Farnsworth said nothing; he simply spread his hands.

I said slowly, "I can't assess the risks because I don't know the North. But there is still work to be done, and I'd like to see us try it. Maybe after today we'll be less foolhardy."

"Bravo," Jayne said. "Fred, how do you feel?"

"I knew it was dangerous when I signed on," the geologist said. "I agree with Mr. Cole—especially on the foolhardiness."

"I'm not voting for going back," Wentz said. "I'm raising the question, that's all. You all have answered it to my satisfaction."

There was a brief silence. I was just beginning to wonder what was going on in Harriet's mind on this subject when the galley door slid back and Harry Chain came in. He was carrying a piece of paper torn off a pad.

"Hi," he said. "The mast works fine and we're in business. I reported back to Alert about the accident—"

"Harry!" Jayne said. "You shouldn't have done that. I was going to file a story on it. Everything you said is in the public domain now—my bosses will have a hæmorrhage."

"Well, I'm sorry, Jayne, but they asked how we were doing and I had to say something, so I told them. Also I've got a message here for Mr. Cole." He handed the paper to me.

I read it twice. It meant the same thing the second time through as it had the first. Everyone was watching me curiously.

"It's from the IGY Committee," I said. "Not from Ellen Fremd this time, but the Committee itself. That wild dispatch you sent from Alert was too much for them to swallow, Jayne. They've disowned us—just as Ellen warned us they would."

"Why, God damn their desiccated heads," Jayne said furiously. "They can't do that."

"They sure as hell can, and they've done it. Now we're in the soup for sure. There's only one chance left for us, and that's to do the work they assigned us to do, and do it *right*."

Farnsworth snorted. "They can take that and shove it, as far as I'm concerned."

"Which is just what they expect you to say. When they hear about our losses, on top of everything else, they'll sympathize for about five minutes—but that'll convince them all over again that we're only a bunch of publicity-happy stumblebums, and probably got just what was coming to us." I knew I was on dangerous ground, but I had had one more shock than I could take; the words kept right on pouring out, regardless. "Nothing will save us now, *nothing*, but going on to the Pole and doing an honest job of work. Otherwise we'll be torn to shreds. Geoffrey, the newspapers will have a field day with this tomorrow; half of them will ridicule us, and the other half will indict us for incompetence running to the edge of manslaughter. After they're through with you, your sponsors won't recognize you when you come back even if you meet them under a klieg light. We've got to do more now than just make it to the Pole and back. We'll have to complete our IGY programme and the rest of our research, and do a bang-up job of it—whether we've got the proper instruments and people for it or not. Otherwise those of us who are still alive will all be destroyed and Wollheim and Benz and Sid and Hanchett will have died for less than nothing."

I discovered that I had been on my feet for some time, though I couldn't remember having stood up. I sat down again, noting with mild surprise that I was shaking.

"By God," Farnsworth said softly. "He's right. Thanks, Julian. I wish you'd been able to convince me sooner, but you sure as hell tried. But maybe it isn't too late. Does anybody have anything to add?"

"Yes," Fred Klein said. "In the eight years that I've known you, Geoffrey, I've never before heard you admit you were wrong. And I think that you're a bigger man for the admission than you could possibly be by being right all the time."

Farnsworth nodded grimly. The meeting hung in stasis for a long second, and then we were all getting up.

I wanted to hit my cabin right away; I was drained dry and I ached from neck to feet. But Wentz stopped me in the companionway.

"That was fine," he said, looking at me with his blood-shot, upsetting eyes, like those of a St. Bernard. "It's been a long time since I last heard a man throw all his emotions right out on the table like that. I'm a lousy old bum without a conviction to my name any more, but by God even I was moved. That took doing."

"Well—thanks, Joe. I surprised myself. I'm glad it helped."

"It was the making of us all. Come on over to the other buggy with me. I've got some baggage to dispose of; we'll have a small party."

My heart sank. I was more than tired; I was disgusted, and astonished that I had enough reserve left to feel anything at all. "No, thanks," I said through a grey fog. "I'm not thirsty, Joe. I just need sleep."

"You don't dig me," the astronomer said. "I'm not thirsty either. I don't want to drink the stuff, I want to burn it, out on the ice. It's mostly brandy. You're the strongest of us all, Julian. I can't do it by myself. Will you help?"

He wasn't pleading. He continued to look at me from under his shaggy eyebrows with an expression that was almost fierce. I knew that the best thing I could do would be to tell him that I trusted him to do the job by himself, but I was too moved to play the all-father, especially to this man who was twice as old as I was and who commanded so many skills I could only admire, never command for myself. There are times when what you know is right feels all wrong, and this was one of them. I said, "Sure, Joe."

And so I spent part of my first "night" on the surface of the Arctic Ocean helping to tend a nearly invisible blue bonfire. It was indeed a party, but such a party as I've attended neither before nor since—half solemn and half gay, like a combination of High Mass and a saint's-day festival on Mulberry Street. We made a puddle first and lit that, and then we took to tossing the bottles in whole, with only the caps off. They would whistle like little rockets until the glass cracked, and then there was a soft explosion as all the rest ignited at once, and the blue fire would rise high enough to make the sky waver.

After a while, Elvers came over from his nearly-completed igloo and squatted down between us, looking at the growing depression in the ice with slow-blinking curiosity. He made my skin crawl, but you don't exclude celebrants from this kind of ceremony.

"Hot," he said at last. "What's the purpose?"

"None at all," Wentz said. His hollow eyes were gleaming. "We just thought we'd like to see a fire."

Elvers nodded, and then went on nodding for what seemed to be a long time, as though his head, once put into motion, had been forgotten while he thought about weightier matters. Then he got up and went away. Though the wind was rising, he was still bare-legged.

"That guy," Wentz said, "gives me the creeps. But he's good with the dogs, I'll give him that."

He uncapped the last bottle and threw it into the fire. The sun had stopped setting and was hovering in the west: midnight. The bottle went *ffffffooosh*-plink, *phung!*

We watched until the flames began to die; then we shook hands and trudged back toward our respective snowmobiles.

Behind us, Elvers was carefully settling into place the capstone of his igloo. It would have no dogs in it after tomorrow.

We had managed to put well over a hundred miles of ice behind us before the disaster, but that left us with nearly four hundred still unaccounted for. Without really stopping to think about it, I had imagined that getting the rest of the way travelled by sled would need weeks, all of them filled with privations I would rather not anticipate. Most of these unformed apprehensions turned out to be wrong, based as they were on nothing more than how much I didn't know about dogsleds and the North.

It's true that a team of dogs makes heavy going of dragging a heavily loaded sled into motion, especially if the sled is carrying not only many full packs, but also a heavy, useless bundle of flesh named Julian Cole. Their blunt claws slip and scrabble and nothing seems to be happening. Once it is actually under way, however, a sled is the closest thing in the world to a frictionless vehicle. As soon as its inertia has been transformed into momentum, pulling it is no problem for seven strong dogs, because it runs not on ice, but on the thin film of water its weight melts as it passes over the ice.

We had not been sliding forward more than two minutes before Wentz had to trot to keep behind the sled. At this point he stepped on to the left runner with one foot, still holding on to the high grips at the back, gave a few pushes with the other foot—for all the world as though making a scooter go—and then was only an additional passenger.

"Mush!"

In all, we did seventy miles on the first day of travel, in three stints of four hours each, with frequent stops of five minutes or so. This, as I found out thereafter, was an unusual distance, and due entirely to the fact that the dogs were fresh; but we made the entire run from snow-mobiles to Pole in six days, which by my figuring means that the dogs averaged about seven miles per working hour, or a little better than that.

Oh, it was a cold, miserable trip, and inexpressibly dreary. In contrast to what I had been expecting, however, it was almost a pleasure, and I would have passed out Dog Yummies every night if I'd had any with me. It was just as well that I didn't. The dogs got fed once a day, after work, and that was that—and they didn't get any igloo to sleep in on the way, either. They slept staked out, well separated so they couldn't get at each other and start fights.

When they weren't working, they were a savage lot, snarling even at Elvers upon very small provocation. He concentrated on keeping on terms of armed truce with the three lead dogs, apparently realizing that it was hopeless to expect the whole pack to be obedient. Even then, in the morning it was Elvers' team that got hitched up first, and then the others. As long as the two trailing teams knew Chinook was leading on the first sled, the subordinate lead dogs would obey Farnsworth and Wentz well enough—especially if they had a chunk of ice thrown at them now and then, and got roared at every few moments. Both Elvers and Farnsworth also had whips, but Elvers seldom used his; as for Wentz, he wouldn't have known how.

The strangest aspect of all this is that the dogs liked it. When Elvers would kick them awake in the morning they would skulk and snarl and snap, but they would head for the first sled all the same, and stand stock still while the traces were being hitched to them. If they tried to take a piece out of Elvers' ear in the process, he cuffed them—and instead of taking his hand off, they would lift a foot to allow a chest strap to go under, or show some other astonishing flash of co-operation. Farnsworth bullied them unmercifully, and they took it, and were working better for him at the end of the six days than I would have imagined possible on the first day.

It was quite different with Wentz. He had no whip, he seldom cuffed, never kicked, never threw things at them. He never had to, because they were afraid of him on sight. If they were co-operative with Elvers and Farnsworth only because they knew that they'd be beaten if they didn't, then it's impossible to account for how they behaved with Wentz. They were afraid of him most of all—and they worked very badly for him, constantly nipping at each other's hocks, pulling free of the traces, ignoring orders, and turning surlily mule-like when we least expected it. When that happened a few good kicks in the ribs from Elvers not only brought them back into line, but somehow made them seem more cheerful (if it's possible for a Malemute to be cheerful).

I think now that, for the dogs, it was a question of knowing who the boss was. Elvers and the Commodore always smelled the same, but Wentz, in the grip of his abrupt withdrawal from alcohol, was untrustworthy: a different man every day to their condemnatory noses.

These dogs are almost all that I remember about our push to the Pole, and I remember that partly because I had my eyes closed against the wind much of the way, and partly because all the fiction about the North I had read when I was a kid had never told me how incredibly noisy a dog-team is while it's working. Eskimo dogs begin to yap and holler the moment they put their shoulders into the straps and start pulling, and they keep it up all day long, no matter how hard the going is. Such a team "talks" like a roomful of Siamese cats, until you wonder how it has any breath left. When I think back to those six days, I "see" very little—a few anonymous men pitching or striking tents, the shapes of sleds, an anomalously hot sun that never went away; but my God, how incessantly that memory barks and barks and barks!

We made it about noon. We had paused to eat somewhere around eleven, and Farnsworth showed his compass around; it was pointing almost due south by Wentz's reckoning. That meant that we were nearly on the plumb line with the magnetic Pole, and couldn't be far away from the geographical Pole. Wentz consulted his clock and his log and did a little quick figuring.

"About ten miles to go," he said.

IX

We were tired, but not exhausted. After another raid on
the E-rations, we got busy putting up the tents and cutting ice. I was assigned to help Wentz build his igloo,
about which he had special ideas: he wanted it so venti-
lated that it was always as cold inside as it was outside,
but at the same time protected from wind and snow. I
thought this a most peculiar taste, and I said so.

"You don't understand telescopes," Wentz said, chipping away at a block which he was holding, tailor-
fashion, in his lap. "It isn't good for them to change
temperature rapidly, for one thing, and for another, they
don't work at all unless they're at the same temperature
as the air they're looking through. If I allowed my
observatory to warm up inside, I'd just have to cool it
down to the outside temperature when I wanted to work
—and the drop here would be so sharp that it might ruin
the optics in the process."

So we built Wentz's igloo with two crossing slits in it,
each one interrupted, necessarily, by the one keystone
ice-block at the summit. Tarps kept the wind and snow
out, except when the instrument—a six-inch Newtonian
reflector—was in use.

"The transpolar satellite must be near launching now,"
I said. "We didn't exactly intend to get up here this late.
Aren't they launching it tomorrow?"

"Yes. But she won't get here until the evening, presuming that she gets into her orbit all right. The equatorial missile was supposed to have been launched four days ago—maybe Harry Chain's heard how that one made out."

"What interests me more is how you're going to see the one that's going over here, with the sun up all the time."

"Oh," said Wentz, "I'll see it, providing they get the co-ordinates up here on time. The trick is partly just knowing where to look. That's up to you; you stick to Jayne until those figures come through and then rush 'em right over to me. What about Minitracking? Is Jayne going to do that?"

"No, I am. I'll get the antenna set up tonight." I paused a moment and then added, "Joe, I don't mean to needle you, but you know how important this is, don't you? We can't afford any flub on it."

Wentz gave me a long, steady look. His trip across the ice had changed him in a great many ways, but individually I found it hard to define them. He looked a little more leathery, a little more alert, a little less sardonic, a little less bloodshot—small changes, and I could not say what it was that I thought they added up to, let alone how well his alcoholic's soul was taking to abstinence. One thing was certain: whatever it was that he had been trying to drown by drinking was back full force, and it was hurting.

"I know what's at stake," he said, and tapped his own chest gently three times. "I don't suppose you ever heard of Wentz's Runaway Giant. A star discovered by another man named Wentz. He's been out of circulation for years. I think I know where he is."

I had blundered, I could see that. That was a button I hadn't meant to touch again; and I made a bad job of pretending I hadn't. I gave him a salute, said, "Roger," and got the hell out of there.

A great deal of work got done during the rest of that day and the succeeding night. You would not believe what eight men and one woman can accomplish in primitive surroundings, and with too few tools, when their lives and their pride depend upon it. No less than four igloos, each of specialized design, were built, and the equipment each was to receive unpacked and installed. Three tents were erected and anchored. Of course, we had no engineer-mechanic any more to man the grapples and the corer, nor any oceanographer either, but we got the igloo built, and the corer and the grapple and winch set up beside it. That would be Farnsworth's baby. The radio shack was for Jayne, and for me; atop it was the dish antenna with which I would catch the satellite's identification signal and feed the co-ordinates into the Minitrack system, if I could; Jayne checked my circuits for me. She turned out to be very good at it, not to my great surprise. The fourth igloo, of course, was for Elvers. It was standard in design, but it was the biggest of the lot, and the strangest noises of the whole expedition came from it.

Wentz took movies of some of the building operations and of the completed camp, and Jayne struck a few poses, but she didn't seem to be enjoying it much, and I'll bet that that stuff would have looked ghastly had we ever gotten around to printing it up. We tried the radio and found that the equatorial satellite had indeed been launched and was a howling success, now circling the

Earth at roughly a thousand miles straight up, in an orbit which varied rhythmically between 40° N. and 40° S. latitude. The Minitrack net along the seventy-fifth meridian was checking it in on schedule.

Mankind had taken the first step into interplanetary space—and where was Julian Cole, science writer, at the time? Why, at the North Pole; where else?

In Florida, the Naval Research Laboratory crew was ready to flash us the co-ordinates of the transpolar moon as soon as it settled into its orbit, which would be about ten minutes after it took off from Cape Canaveral. Harry Chain would then get them to us, and I'd rush them to Wentz in time for him to set them up on his telescope drive.

Harriet was fine, and there was no news. We dossed down.

I was awakened in the morning by the snoring of the grapple engine, and discovered again one of the singular advantages of sleeping in virtually unheated surroundings in a permanent winter: you never have to get out of bed into the cold. When you get up, so does the bed—you're wearing it.

I wandered into the radio igloo, where Jayne had managed coffee; everyone was there, except Elvers, who was so often absent from such gatherings that I had almost stopped noticing it. It was warm enough inside for me to slip my hood back, and we all talked at once—I don't remember about what. Then Farnsworth left to resume his blind groping on the floor of the Arctic Ocean. He had already brought up two cores, but apparently they had contained nothing exciting; I recall his remarking that he'd used them to fill our quota of soil samples for Pfistner. The mention of Pfistner reminded me belatedly of another loss that we had sustained with the first snowbuggy: a bundle of first-day covers that Pfistner's Will Claflin, an ardent philatelist, had consigned to us for cancellation at the Pole. Claflin had put up the money out of his own pocket, and had published an article about it in one of the major collectors' magazines. Obviously there was no point in bringing this up now; in fact, it even amused me, for stamp-collecting has always struck me as only the next best thing to lint-picking.

The rest of us got at the thousand-headed chore of just keeping the camp in operation. There were no real hitches. Even the satellite's flight over the Pole was unremarkable, though it did cause a brief flash of alarm. I never saw it, of course, but what was more important, I never did get any signal from it, though Cape Canaveral reported it launched on schedule, orbital height 676 miles, etc., and Harry Chain got every necessary figure to us at the Pole within minutes after he received the relay from Alert. I ran the figures to Wentz, and tracked along them faithfully myself, but no signal came through.

Full of apprehension, I ran back to Wentz's igloo. He laughed in my face.

"We got it cold," he said. "The radio transmitter in it must have cut out, that's all. Nine gravities of acceleration are hard on instruments. But it came right up over the horizon, right on schedule, going like a bat out of hell, and I had it dead centre in my field of view for about forty degrees. I would have had more, if I'd been able to run the 'scope outdoors, but not in this wind; there would have been too much tremble. The seeing was lousy as it was."

"Did you get the figures?"

"Sure. Here they are—send 'em on." He grinned suddenly. "I also got five plates. There's nothing we can do with 'em here, but once we get back to Farnsworth's snowbuggy we can develop them and nail the thing down to within three seconds of arc, maybe closer."

"Well, thank God. Good for you, Joe. I was scared for a minute there. I never got a peep out of it, and I was tracking it along the same co-ordinates, I'm positive."

"Radio astronomy," Wentz said solemnly, "will never replace the horse." And again he tapped his own chest.

"What are you going to do next?"

"I'm going to start spotting emulsions all over the snow around here. We've lost Hanchett, but *somebody* has to do the cosmic-ray work. Who knows, maybe there's an anti-chronon or two scooting around here waiting to be trapped. I'm a little rusty at that stuff; time I got back into practice."

He pinned the tarps back up very carefully, put a dew-cap over the business end of his telescope, stowed his oculars away in their velvet-lined cases, and began to unpack foil-covered photographic plates out of a small, lead-lined box. I doubted that anything would come of this operation, for the plates couldn't have been part of Hanchett's equipment; and if they were Wentz's, they were old, and hence useless. Emulsions for cosmic-ray work preferably should be prepared on the spot and used within twenty-four hours; cosmic rays, especially the heavy primaries, go through an ordinary lead lining as though it were cheese. Nevertheless, I was more than satisfied, and I left Wentz happily programming his experiment.

I went back to the radio igloo and had Jayne put Wentz's figures on the air toward home, and then walked the necessary half-mile to see what Farnsworth was up to. He was out in the open, squatting over a glistening fifteen-foot cylinder about four inches in diameter, which he was splitting longitudinally with an ordinary paring-knife. It was, of course, a core—a thin cylinder of oozes and clays brought up from the ocean floor. It was remarkably colourful, each layer of sediment carrying its own chalky whiteness, or mustard-yellow, or mauve or brick-red or blue; here and there, too, a layer was marbled with another colour.

Farnsworth didn't seem to notice me, so I watched silently. He was now cutting the core like a long loaf of bread, into a series of chunks, each one representing one stratum. He had almost reached the bottom end of the core when he grunted like a man who has been struck. The blunt nose of the paring-knife dug into the stiff mud and flicked something out into Farnsworth's hand. After looking at it a moment, he rolled it energetically in the snow to clean it, and then held it up to the sun.

In so doing, he saw me. "Hello, Julian. Did we get the satellite?"

"Joe Wentz got it. I missed it clean. I don't think it was signalling by the time it went over us, but Joe got photos. What have you got, Geoffrey?"

"Jackpot. Take a look."

When I was young, a girl I was going with shocked me profoundly by quoting at a party the article in the old

Britannica about the testicle, which it described as being "about the size and shape of a plover's egg". To a chorus of outraged laughter, she had said: "Well, now we know how big a plover's egg is."

The object Farnsworth handed me was about the size and shape of a plover's egg. It was made of dark brown glass, and its surface was etched into a series of crawling, rounded ridges, like copulating worms. I had never seen anything like it before, but I knew enough now to be suspicious of odd bits of glass. I said:

"This is a tektite?"

"Right," Farnsworth said. "I pulled this core from about seventy-five feet below the surface of the ocean bottom. Evidently there's never been a turbidity current this far north; I haven't found any traces of sand or gravel, so the bottom can't have been silted over under the ice-cap since the cap last reformed. This is a part of the original fall, just as I'd hoped."

I turned it over in the unvarying sky-glare. "What are these worms all over the surface of it?"

"Water erosion. That's what all tektites look like if they've been imbedded in wet soil since they fell. The glass is slightly soluble, you see."

He was elated, that was obvious. I could hardly blame him.

"What next?" I said.

"Well, I'm going to have to date it pretty closely. I get only a rough date from the clay-layer I found it in. With the microscope, I can check the matrix for shells, but I'm not enough of a biologist to learn much from that; I'll take photomicrographs home and let the experts do that part of the work. Maybe they can get a better date by

Libby's radio-carbon system, too. But above all, I want more tektites, so I can be sure there was a major fall here when the protoplanet broke up. That much, at least, is a certainty."

"Why?"

"Because I found this one so quickly," Farnsworth said patiently. "The odds are hugely against my hitting one this early, unless the substrata around here are literally riddled with tektites. If I get confirmation, I'll drop the grapple and see what we can bring up with a really big bite out of the bottom."

"You'd do that anyhow," I pointed out.

"To be sure," he said, grinning like a small boy. "But it'd be pleasant to be doing it with some assurance that there's something down there to grapple for. Come now, Julian, you're more than three-quarters convinced already; admit it. You could even give me a hand, if you like." He stood up, a little creakily.

"*Euer Gnaden, zu Befehl.*"

"Eh? Oh. Very good. Let's take some of these sections into the igloo."

So I got down on my hands and knees and crawled. Unfortunately, there is no other way to enter an igloo. Farnsworth pocketed a number of the oozing hemi-cylinders he had cut from the core and came huffing down the truncated entrance tunnel after me.

The light inside the igloo was dim and just barely adequate, for only enough light from the overcast sky was transmitted by the blocks of compressed snow to provide a sort of pearly twilight inside. On a low bench, Farnsworth had a few basic tools set up—a microscope, a scleroscope, a balance, some small bottles of reagents with etched labels. There was also a tripod with a pot sitting on it, under which a can of Sterno flickered with dismal blue-violet. I pointed to it.

"Coffee?"

"No, just water. It won't stay liquid otherwise, you know." Well, I'd have realized it if I'd thought about it a moment longer, I suppose. The trouble, of course, was that I was still not used to thinking in terms of permanent sub-freezing temperatures, indoors and out. Farnsworth spread his core-sections on the bench, and then chucked the one in which he'd found the tektite into the pot.

"Like to screen these?" he said. "What you can do, Julian, is to keep stirring that mess until the matrix is evenly dispersed. Then pour it all off through the mesh here, and give me anything that stays behind. Then you put a chunk of ice in the pot and we do it all over again with the next segment."

He heated a short length of metal rod over the flaming jellied alcohol until it was glowing, and then plunged it at an angle into the wall of the igloo just above the bench. After three such operations—each one producing a screaming hiss—he had holed through, and there was a little patch of unobstructed daylight on the surface of the bench. I continued to stir, watching puzzledly until he slid the microscope into a position where he could catch the incoming light on the instrument's substage mirror.

"Have to do that almost every hour," he said abstractedly. "Just breathing in here makes the bore frost closed." He heated a slide briefly, pipetted a few drops of the sludge from the pot on to it, and slipped it on to the microscope stage.

"What's to keep your little puddle from freezing?"

"Well, it's got sea water mixed in with it, of course," he said. "But it'll freeze soon enough, all the same. Hmm. . . . Globeriginae. That's logical. Wish I knew them by species."

My own mud-puddle seemed to be completed now, so I picked up the pot with a pair of tongs and poured the contents into a slop-bucket through the piece of fine screening Farnsworth had indicated. Sure enough, several small solid bits remained on the screen.

"Geoffrey?"

"Mmm?"

"You'll have to pardon the implication, but—you seem to know pretty well what you're doing."

His head came up from the microscope like a shot at that, and I got the benefit of a 250-watt Farnsworth glare.

"What the hell, man," he said. "I've been all over the world, and all my treks have had *some* scientific purpose or other—sometimes many at once, like this one. Do you think people hand out such jobs to total idiots?"

"I guess I thought so until pretty recently, in your case at least," I admitted. "You do act like an idiot, when you're not at work."

"The world is full of newspapermen whose attention can't be captured by anything else," he said. "If you don't act like an idiot they'll turn you into one anyhow. I remember an incident back in the thirties, when the high-and-mighty American Rocket Society was still in its infancy. They ran some kind of a proving-stand test on a small engine, out on Long Island, one Sunday afternoon. It yielded quite a lot of data. But all the ARS members in those days were just dedicated amateurs, for all that many of them were engineers—they had to be amateurs, because there wasn't any such thing as a profession of rocketry in those days, at least not in this country.

"So the next day, the New York *Ledger Columbian* gave the test a two-column box on its front page, headlined, 'Shot At Moon Is Fizzle'. Of course, it wasn't a shot at the Moon, or at any place; the engine was tied down to the proving-stand. The text of the story was supposed to be funny. That's the kind of reporter whose attention I have to capture—because it's publicity that pays for my expeditions, and because the projects I try to investigate are just as off-trail these days as rocketry was back then, so I'm not respectable. I have to make a fool of myself to keep the press from making fools of my sponsors, and making a mock of my projects. And for what? Do you think that reporter ever went back to Larry Manning and Ed Pendray and the rest of that little hard core of rocketry experimenters and apologized for that verminous story? Did it enter his mind when the V-2s began falling on London? Of course not. That same reporter is probably now yellow-paging one or another of those same men as suspected 'Reds' who *might* give away vital rocketry secrets to Russia. That's the kind of paper he works for, and that's the kind of reporter he is."

He stopped and looked down at the little pool of mud on the microscope slide. Even from where I was standing, I could see that it had turned a dirty yellow; it had frozen while he was talking. He looked back at me.

"What's more," he said through his teeth, "you're another."

I stood there and took it. The National Association of Science Writers might have expected its past president to make him a rebuttal speech about how much more responsible science reporting has become since the thirties, but it never even crossed my mind. Because, you see, I knew he was right.

And suddenly, paradoxically, I wasn't sorry any more that I'd been at the North Pole when the greatest science story since nuclear fission had broken. Right here in this Sterno-stinking foggy little igloo, standing in my sweaty furs, melting a lump of ice to make another mud-puddle like the one that had stained the ice in brown spatters around the slop-bucket, I was beginning—just beginning—to learn my trade.

Evidently my expression must have been openly stricken. Farnsworth took the slide from under the microscope's stage clips and set it aside. "I can melt the damned thing again," he said gruffly. "Let's see what you've got there on the screen. Here's another chunk for the pot."

We swapped. I put the new piece of core in the pot, and he set the screen on the bench and turned the small irregular objects on it over with a pencil-point.

There was quite a long silence; and then, almost under his breath, he muttered:

"Sorry."

"Forget it," I said hoarsely. "Find anything?"

"No. These are just ordinary igneous rock, very much water-worn. There are two little shards that might be tektites, but they're too small to identify except chemically. And that's all. Let's try it again."

We tried it again, and then again. Nothing came out

but pebbles, until the fourth try, when we found one other inarguable, wormy-surfaced tektite, about half the size of the first. Farnsworth was mildly pleased, but he grumbled all the same; it could have been a coincidence.

After that, his luck appeared to have deserted him completely, and after the ninth or tenth sample had come out of the pot he snuffed the Sterno can and just sat in front of the bench for a while, poking moodily at the motley collection of pebbles. He seemed to have a pet hate among them: a pock-marked, forlorn bit of rock about as big as his first tektite, but not half as pretty. Finally he picked it up and glared at it, as though attempting to will it out of existence. It seemed so lost in the palm of his heavy glove that for a moment I thought he'd gotten his wish.

"What the hell," he said disgustedly.

I didn't really know what to say, but keeping my mouth shut is not one of my talents. "As a matter of fact, Geoffrey," I said, "I think your luck's been excellent, for this early in the game. Two tektites and two possibles in one sampling operation——"

"Shut up," he said suddenly. "I'm sorry, but by the living Buddha, look at this. And it was right under my nose all the time!"

"What? What is it?"

He ignored me; suddenly, he was all arms. He took a hardness test on the pebble, and swore at the scleroscope for not being a Rockwell tester. He sampled his pebble and ran chemical tests, and swore at his reagent shelf for not being the complete warehouse stock of Otto Greiner & Co. He rubbed grains off it and scowled at them through the microscope. At one point, he put a drop of something or other on the pebble and *smelled* it, which made him sneeze and swear like a top sergeant.

Then he sat down and just stared at the pebble. By this time, I was holding my breath, but he didn't seem to know I was there. He just turned the pebble over and over again in his fingers.

"Geoffrey, what the hell? What is it?"

"It's what I've been looking for—or part of it," he said in a husky voice. "It's the last bit, the inner core, of a meteorite made of *sedimentary* rock. It's the very first such meteorite ever discovered. When I think of how long it's been lying down there, dissolving away. . . ."

His voice trailed off shakily. He got up, opened the Sterno can and lit it again. "It goes into a paraffin block, right now—no, there's too much helium in paraffin. Let's see; better make it ordinary ice. My God—cosmic history in an ice-cube! What a break!"

I was just about to say, *Are you sure?* when I realized that *I* was sure. I said instead, "But what does it mean?"

"It means," Farnsworth said gently, "that meteorites come from some place in the solar system where there was once a large body of water in the liquid state. Ergo, the asteroidal protoplanet—or one of them—was Earth-like at one time. It supported seas, over a long geological period. It was warm then, warmer than Mars—which means that it had an atmosphere too, and a thick one, as thick as Earth's; so it must have been bigger than the Earth. And it means that it was destroyed within the lifetime of man."

He looked at me levelly for a moment more, and then added:

"It also means, Julian, that there's more of it down

134

below, where there's been less water in the soil—but still quite close to the bottom. I'm going to bring up some substantial bits of it on the first grab. What are you going to tell your friend Ellen Fremd and those pinheads at the IGY? Or the newspapers, for that matter?"

I didn't know; I had to spread my hands helplessly.

"I can suggest a headline," Farnsworth said. " 'Shot At Stars Is Dribble' would be standard, wouldn't it?"

It was at that moment, I think now, that I really began to hate him. I had no other choice; he was getting too close to home.

X

Since I couldn't talk to Harriet without the whole world hearing what we said, at least potentially, I had to sweat it out all by myself. As it turned out, I had plenty of time, for that night the overcast sky turned to mud, and it began to snow. The fall took less than half an hour to turn into a blizzard, and the blizzard went on for nearly a week, as though the whole notion of snow had just been conceived and the Powers wanted to know how far it could be pushed. At long last I had darkness aplenty.

During the first three or four hours of that howling maelstrom, I thought of nothing at all but what I was doing, and I'm sure nobody else had any time for philosophical questions, either. The tents were ballooning alarmingly in the wind, which ran up to forty miles an hour even then, and we had to secure them with deep-driven pitons along every margin, and rig new guy-wires to keep their telescopic masts from toppling. The coring and grappling rigs were too heavy to be in danger from the wind, but they were going to be buried in the snow, and there was nothing we could do about that but spike tarps over them; we simply lacked the manpower to heave them into any sort of shelter, and we couldn't hitch up the dogs to help us on this short notice. Staggering in the gusts, leaning against the wind when it was steady, almost totally blind, we got everything inside that would go inside, and after that there was nothing we could do but wait it out, nursing our raw faces.

Wentz and I spent that night in the same tent we had been sharing since we had arrived, but it was no longer a tent; it was a huge and menacing jellyfish. The walls of it fluttered like eardrums; the wires howled and sang; the mast thrummed. The heat-reflective aluminium foil-cloth lining was almost no good at all, because it was impossible to keep the wind from blowing around the edges of the entrance-flaps and carrying the radiant heat off as fast as it accumulated. Only the Davy stove kept us from freezing that week, along with the pressure lamp we lit when we got up in the morning. That burned kerosene and put out considerable heat—enough to make it go off like a bomb if we goaded it too far. But it was better than the flying ice and snow, no matter how dangerous it was. Outside, the temperature was minus 34° and still falling. Had the tent been ripped away over us while we slept, we would have frozen without waking, as fast as a Birdseye flounder.

And so I had nothing to do but either prepare myself for death—a project I could not advance one inch before having to abandon it to a blind determination to see Midge and the kids again—or else think about the portentous pebble at the heart of Farnsworth's ice-cube. The noise and the slashing cold made it impossible to talk to Wentz except in snatches of two or three words, and he seemed to begrudge even that; I don't think the storm bothered him much, but something was on his mind; we lived through that siege like deaf-mutes. So I huddled, and thought.

I got nowhere. Like it or not, I believed Farnsworth's

protoplanet notion now, and it didn't matter that I was beginning to dislike him personally. That pebble in the ice-cube was *important*—it was, in fact, a great discovery, and there would be confirmation to follow if we all lived through this inferno of ice. And it was up to me, as the closest thing the expedition had left to a reputable observer, to report the discovery back——

—which would cut my throat, ruin the expedition finally and completely, and insure that the discovery itself would be added to the long list of historic scientific hoaxes: Piltdown Man, the Cardiff Giant, bioflavenoids for colds, dianetics, the Moon Hoax, whatever it had been that Wentz had pulled, the Haeckel scandal, the saucer craze, Lysenkoism, ESP, antihistamines for colds, *Salamandra*, Orson Welles' Martians, scientology, the chlorophyll boom . . . a long list, and due to grow longer as the years grew. There would be no sense in contributing another term to that open-ended series, even if the term were indeed a fact.

No reputable scientist would dare to believe a word out of Farnsworth's expedition now. The best that he could hope for was to become another of the Fortean Society's pre-lost causes. Bad means had totally corrupted good ends.

And yet, and yet . . . Farnsworth's discovery was important. If I failed to report it back, I was through—not at home, but inside my own skin. As for home, wasn't I through there already? I couldn't possibly serve as historian to the IGY for an expedition that wasn't IGY any longer; nor would Pierpont-Millennium-Artz be likely to accept a book about the expedition from me now that the IGY tie-in was dead. The second book

Artz might have taken was of course already out of the question, and so was any marginal income I might have made from magazine and newspaper articles about the trip. Most of the periodical space had already been soaked up by the public relations shops of Farnsworth's sponsors, and that was all free copy; I couldn't hope to get paid for more of the same, unless I told the truth, which would destroy us all. The best that I could hope for was to get back home more than seven thousand dollars in debt—and I knew better now, than to hope to get off so easily.

I slept badly.

The snow slackened off at the end of the second day of the storm, but that was hard to detect for a while. The winds kept on blowing, picking up the little needles and pouring them in horizontal torrents along the white air. We were still pinned down, and our kerosene was almost gone; we gave up the pressure lantern and lived in darkness, nursing the oven. It was so cold that we couldn't even smell each other, though we both stank mightily, as I was reminded by the puff of air out of my neckline each time I sat or lay down. On the third day, the wind dropped abruptly to about fifteen miles per hour, the temperature rose to five above zero, and it began snowing all over again, great fat flakes like those common in temperate-zone winters.

I found that I could talk to Wentz again, and I took full advantage of it to tell him what was on my mind. His face was sallow as he listened; now and then he coughed.

"I can't help you," he said when I was through. "Maybe later. We're out of fuel, Julian; we can get to the radio igloo on a line, if you want to try it."

"Sure. Right away. I'll be glad to get out of this trap. But Joe, I've got one more question—and you can tell me it's none of my damn business if you want to. I wouldn't ask if I didn't think it was pertinent."

"I don't know," he said, his glance straying slowly to the floor. "I'll try, Julian. That's the best I can do."

"Good for you. What I want to know is: What was Wentz's Runaway Giant? Was that what they cashiered you for, and why they took away your degree? Was it *really* a hoax, or did they frame you?"

He looked out from under his hood at me with suffused eyes, and the most frightening expression I had ever seen.

"Hands off," he said. "It was no hoax, but. . . . *Hands off*, that's all."

Good advice, and I should have taken it—but I may never learn to keep my mouth shut. I said, "Then it's a real star, Joe?"

Wentz coughed until he choked and had to turn away. After a second or so he said in a strangled voice, "It's not in the catalogue. Let me alone, can't you?"

"Sure, Joe, I'm sorry." I put myself together and pulled my goggles down over my eyes. "Hold the fort; I'll be back."

He nodded, still without looking at me, and got his pack out from behind his bedding. He was still working on the straps when I ducked out into the whirling snowstorm.

I found the line that led to the radio igloo after only a minute of groping, but in that minute I came close to dying. There was no East or West, no North or South, hardly any up or down—there wasn't even any time out there. Every atom of the whole world was in white motion around me, and I had the illusion that I could feel it turning on its axis underneath me. Without the line, I would have staggered in circles until I froze.

Once I hit it, I crawled along it as blindly as though I were an aerialist sliding down a wire, suspended only from a rubber bit between his teeth. I knew damn well I shouldn't be trying it by myself, not even over this short a distance and on a guide-line; but Wentz certainly had made no move to go along with me, despite the fact that it had been he who had made the initial suggestion, and I wanted to talk to Jayne too badly to wait his mood out. The trip lasted only a little short of for ever.

Then I was emerging inside the igloo, on my hands and knees. It was warm and light in there, but I was going to have no chance to talk to Jayne. Her husband was with her, and so was Fred Klein, who was Farnsworth's tentmate—I did not then know why. Both the Farnsworths were wearing earphones and intent expressions; Fred was standing on a packing box, inspecting the circuits on my Minitrack antenna. He saw me first.

"Here's Julian now," he said, climbing down. "You did a good job here, Julian. I can't find anything wrong, at least. There just wasn't any damn satellite to track—that's the answer."

"No satellite? But Joe Wentz——"

"God only knows what Wentz saw. Pink terns, maybe."

"That," I said, "is a damn lie, Fred. He's off the stuff entirely. If he says he saw it, he saw it. Hell, he even got pictures of it!"

"Have you seen them, Julian?" Jayne said grimly.

"Yes. Well, I haven't seen anything but the plates; he

can't develop them here. But what's going on here, anyhow? I thought we were all through with that satellite hassel."

Farnsworth took off the earphones and gave me a long look. "I don't really think it makes a nickel's worth of difference anyhow," he said. "But Joe missed it clean, Julian. Look here."

He handed me a piece of paper torn from a scratch pad. I was getting to hate those chits—and sure enough, this one carried the same kind of bad news that the one I'd gotten from Harry Chain had, back at the base camp. It said:

ATTN 2WPBE COMMANDANT STOP FIGURES YOU SUPPLIED FOR TRANSPOLAR SATELLITE TRANSIT CORRELATE CLOSELY BY CHI-SQUARE TEST WITH ROUTE OF DAILY STOCKHOLM-TOKYO FLIGHT INAUGURATED 1955 BY SCANDINAVIAN AIRLINES STOP NO VISUAL OR MINITRACK OBSERVERS AVAILABLE TO CONFIRM INSIDE EMERGENT CONE THIS UNPREDICTED TRAJECTORY STOP PLEASE RECONFIRM AND VERIFY WITH PREDICTIONS IF POSSIBLE SIGNED WHIPPLE IGY VANGUARD

My heart sank. I had, I knew, been expecting something of exactly this sort . . . and yet at the same time I couldn't even begin to believe it.

"This can't be Joe's fault," I said. "He picked the thing up just where they said it would cross over us. And he had the telescope on it all the way—he *couldn't* have mistaken an airliner's lights for a celestial object. Airliner riding lights blink, for Christ's sake—and why would an SAS plane be flying riding lights in the summer here anyhow?"

"Don't ask me," Farnsworth said. "Maybe he just caught the glare off the side or the wings. He's the very man to do it. I'm just as pleased that it worked out this way, anyhow. We tried, we missed, and that's that. Now we can get down to business."

"Geoffrey, you're out of your mind. Why won't you give him a chance? Who's going to believe in your sedimentary meteorite, if you allow Joe to be discredited? Don't you *want* to be believed?"

"I don't think it will make a particle of difference one way or the other," Farnsworth said disgustedly. "The meteorite is inarguably just what it is. I've had Fred working on it, and he confirms my views." I looked at the geologist, who nodded—a little reluctantly, I thought, but perhaps I only imagined it. "What difference can it make whether or not Joe got squiffed and missed their damned tin can? They expected to lose half of them, anyhow, didn't they?"

"Joe wasn't drunk. He doesn't have anything with him *to* drink. I saw him burn it all, myself. As for the satellite, the IGY wants its course plotted because any deviation it shows from prediction will help provide evidence for the true shape of the Earth. In other words, they're charting the Earth's gravitational field—which governed the course your meteorite followed as it fell. That in turn will be a clue to where it came from." I didn't at all know whether or not this was true; I was counting on Geoffrey's not knowing, either. "Anyhow, that's all beside the point. You're not even giving Joe a chance—that's what counts. You're the guy who dragged him up here, and took advantage of his being down on his luck—and now that it looks like he's in more trouble, you're all set to ditch him without even listening to him. Is that what you call being a human being?"

"In a minute I'm going to lose my temper," Farnsworth said edgily. "This is no country for being free with dangerous accusations, Julian."

"Agreed," I retorted. "And you're being mighty free about accusing Joe of fluffing. Why won't you give him a chance?"

"Oh, all right. I'll talk to him. It can't do any harm."

"Good. Come on then. You can help me haul some fuel back."

"In *this* weather?" the Commodore said. "I'll talk to him, Julian, but stop pushing. He'll keep, after all."

Jayne stood up. "I'll go, Geoffrey," she said. "Think it over while I'm gone. Maybe it won't pay to be bull-headed this time. It didn't pay before."

He scowled at her, but offered no objections.

"Thanks," I told her. "Geoffrey, do me the favour of remembering that you admitted I was right the last time. Believe me, this thing is the very last blow as far as the expedition's prestige is concerned—unless Joe really saw that satellite and can prove it, pix and all."

"Julian," Farnsworth growled, "*stop pushing*. Don't you ever recognize when you've won an argument?"

Alarmed, I shut up and got to work.

Jayne helped me drag the fuel-cans willingly enough, but it seemed to take hours. Out in the open there was a complete "whiteout"—an even glare of daylight on flying snow and ice-crystals which obliterated not only the horizon but the very distinction between the ground and the sky, so that our vision was as useless as if we had been crawling with pillow-cases over our heads. By the time we got back to the tent we were nearly snowblind despite our goggles, and stumbled and bumped into each other and against anonymous objects, and spilled kerosene on the ground trying to load the stove and the lantern until I was almost afraid to strike a match to make them go. At last, however, the stove thumped softly and began to compete with the all-pervasive cold; and a moment later, another pop, a droning hiss and a glare of yellow light announced that Jayne had gotten the lantern into operation.

At first, even after my eyes got used to the new change in illumination, I failed almost completely to understand what I saw. The inside of the tent was a shambles, but not at all the kind of shambles that might have been explained in terms of the storm. My first wild assumption was that a polar bear had broken into the place, though we had yet to see one.

The whole floor of the tent was littered with scraps and wads of paper, and with large, rectangular pieces of grey glass, on one of which somebody had stepped—probably Jayne, since I didn't remember having crunched down on anything while we were groping. There were also wads of aluminium foil, and a good many scattered heaps of clothing, all the latter apparently from Wentz's pack, which had been torn open.

Then I saw Wentz. He was lying on his sleeping bag— not in it—with his eyes open, staring cloudily at the pinnacle of the tent. His mouth was open, his breathing loud and bubbling.

"Joe! Joe!"

"It's no use, Julian," Jayne said, with a sort of amused regret. "I've seen it all before. The first time we took Joe

Wentz on safari with us, he had only one piece of luggage with him—containing one change of clothing, a bottle of Scotch, a bottle of rye, a bottle of gin, a bottle of dry vermouth, a bottle of sour mash bourbon, a bottle of brandy, a bottle of perfume, a bottle of ink and a bottle of ketchup. Geoffrey was right; he never changes."

"It can't be. He must be sick." I dropped to my knees beside him and bent to listen to his chest.

We were, as it turned out, both right. He was drunk, without doubt; this close to him I could smell the stuff. After a moment of rummaging, I even found the bottle: a half-litre of straight ethyl alcohol, either from our medical stores or from Farnsworth's or Fred's stock of reagents. It still contained an oozing lump of cloudy crystals about as big as my fist. I was obscurely glad to discover that it wasn't whisky—or perfume, for that matter—though the fact made Wentz not one whit less drunk.

But he was sick, too. It didn't take much guessing to figure out what was the matter with him—not in this country, and with Wentz's history.

Like most long-confirmed alcoholics, he was a push-over for pneumonia.

I handed Jayne the empty flask without comment. "He's got so much congestion in his chest now that he's damn near drowning," I said huskily. "Now's our chance to see if all that tabascomycin Pfistner gave us is as good as they said it was. Drunk or sober, we've got to bail him out of this—to save his life, *and* to hear what his story is on this satellite foul-up."

She nodded and looked around; I pointed out our first-aid bundle.

146

"Are you in any doubt about the story?" she said, gently.

"I sure as hell am. So, all right, he's drunk now, that's plain to see. But I *know* he wasn't drunk during the satellite transit. If he's back on the stuff now, it's nobody's fault but mine."

"Really, Julian?" she said. "Oh hell, this is one of Pfistner's Mechaniject syringes—I keep forgetting how you open them. . . . Ah, there it is. I can't quite see you pouring raw alcohol down him against his will."

"That isn't what I mean." I wasn't entirely sure what I did mean, for that matter; all I had was a gnawing suspicion, and I was fighting that as hard as I could. I felt for Wentz's pulse; it was way up, and his forehead was burning.

Jayne loaded the syringe with a cartridge like a professional and knelt beside us. "Rump or arm?" I asked her.

"Just roll up his sleeve. He's chilled enough already without taking his pants down." She sank the needle into his triceps muscle with the neat precision of a marksman placing a dart, and the plunger went home. I swabbed the puncture with the drippings from the alcohol bottle and rolled Wentz's sleeve back down.

"Are you a nurse too, Jayne?"

"Hell no," she said abstractedly, lifting the sick astronomer's eyelids and looking under them. Deprived of its forced animation, her face, I could see now, was so rounded in contour as to be downright motherly; her professional photographs had given her bone-highlights that she just didn't have when her face was relaxed. "But in the jungle everybody has to know how to give shots, if you want to keep your bearers. . . . He's damn sick, all right. . . . Even the healthiest boys can turn up with tropical ulcers between one day's trek and another. We used to burn penicillin like gin, some weeks."

She settled him into his bedding, and sat down on mine to watch him. There was, of course, nothing else that could be done for a while but watch.

I couldn't stay still, all the same, and instead I began to pick compulsively about in the litter. The scraps and wads of paper turned out to be reprints from an issue of *Astronomica Acta*, dated ten years ago. They were all headed:

AN N-CLASS HIGH-LUMINOSITY STAR
SHOWING HIGH PROPER MOTION
A Preliminary Report
J. Wentz
(Ph. D., Utrecht)

Evidently he had had a cache of the pamphlets in his pack along with the filched alcohol—and had been spending his time since I had seen him last drinking and brooding over his paper. The year-date was right for the year his honorary doctorate from Lisbon had been both awarded and revoked; God only knew what that meant. But it was clear that before he had passed out, he had begun to destroy the copies one after another, but had not been able to bring himself to do a complete job of it. In the end, the lantern must have gone out while he was still at it; the four undamaged pamphlets I found fanned out at the foot of the bedding must have evaded his groping hands in the frigid darkness.

Thereafter, he had had no choice but to sit alone in

the invisible wreckage, thinking about Wentz's Runaway Giant, and sucking the sludge from the ice crystals through the neck of the bottle. After a while, he had groped about for something else to destroy, and had found it: the pieces of glass on the floor.

They were photographic plates, deprived of their covers, which were also amid the litter. The aluminium foil belonged to the cosmic-ray emulsions; the red-and-black paper sheets to the optical plates; he had missed neither. I suppose that, even in his fury of self-loathing, he had not begun to strip the plates until after the lantern sputtered out and left him in the cold darkness, but it did us no good to speculate about that now; for even had the plates been safe as long as the tent had been dark, they had been exposed the moment that Jayne had lit the lantern.

Possibly the cosmic-ray emulsions were still salvageable; with them it wasn't the surface exposure that counted, but the deep penetrating of particles millions of times more massive than light-photons. Had Hanchett been with us still, he would have known what to do for them, if anything could indeed still be done.

But the optical plates were kaput. We were never going to know whether Joe had photographed the IGY's satellite, or just a high-flying SAS airliner. His say-so was all we had left. The evidence lay wiped out around our feet.

Under the twin drives of the stove and the lamp, the tent began to warm up. The winds that were creating the whiteout were turbulent, but they were no match for those that we had had during the storm proper; the tent was reasonably heat-tight again, and the foilcloth reflected the warmth back at us in increasing waves. It felt good for a while, and then it began to feel a little like too much of a good thing; but we didn't stop it down. Wentz needed it. Sick, drunk and bedraggled as he was, he couldn't be allowed to sweat out his fever inside his work-clothes—Jayne had already stripped him of those —and his occasional violent starts invariably burst him halfway out of his bedding. We had to make sure that he wasn't exposed to the raw winter each time he thrashed himself uncovered.

But it got more and more uncomfortable for us. I gave up first, peeling myself out of my parka. This left me walking about in the same outfit—twill shorts and flight jacket—that I had ridiculed when I had first seen Elvers wearing it out in the open on the ice-cap; I didn't think it so funny now. Jayne held out a little longer, and when she emerged from her snowsuit I could understand why: she was wearing a tight-fitting, astonishingly shaggy red wool union-suit. Under any other circumstances, I would either have goggled or dissolved into helpless laughter; she was a caricature of every calendar cheesecake picture ever painted, and for that matter I looked pretty bizarre myself. But we neither of us laughed. I remember thinking only that the whiteout was for once in our favour, since as long as it lasted neither Farnsworth nor anybody else would be likely to blunder in and see us in these Beaux-Arts rigs.

"Do you think we can take turns sleeping?" I asked her.

"I don't think so, Julian. Listen to that cough—if it gets any worse he'll strangle in his own sputum unless one of us is around to catch him when the crisis comes. If he wakes up, we'll have to give him water, and some broth if possible. And in any event he'll have to have another shot every four hours around the clock. We'll each of us have to help keep the other one awake—and in this heat it isn't going to be easy."

"Then we'd better eat, ourselves."

I broke out rations, and Jayne made a thick, anonymous soup of them atop the stove. It was pleasant to have a hot meal, even though the fumes from the stove and the lantern masked out most of its taste; it was authoritatively salty, and that was all, but at least it was also hot. Then we squatted down, side by side, to watch Joe.

I was beginning to nod when Jayne said suddenly: "Fred's the last we have, isn't he, Julian?"

"Um? The last what?"

"The last real scientist. We're about cashiered, as far as scientific standing is concerned—even if we pull Joe through."

"Just what I've been saying," I said, resting my chin on my knees. Jayne stretched her legs out in front of her and leaned back.

"All right. We're going to be mud with our sponsors when we get back, I can see that. But Julian, I can't make Geoffrey see it. Oh, he believes it off the top of his head, but he isn't really sold on it. He thinks that if he can just get back home with his pieces of protoplanet, people are going to forgive him everything and fall on his neck with glad cries."

"They won't."

"I know they won't," she said, sitting up again with sudden energy. "They'll laugh him to death—maybe even get him up before an inquest for losing the people in the snowbuggy. But he just doesn't give a damn. I know how he is when he's cut off from home, and finds something he thinks is going to make him a publicity saint—or thinks he's found something. He won't listen to me, let alone anybody else. Once he sees the limelight coming around in his direction, he breaks his arms elbowing everybody else out into the wings. He can't stand sharing the glory; he's wild for it—*all* of it."

She shook her hair out and glared at me as though I were responsible. I was awake again, but I could think of no suitable response, or indeed any response at all. The fumes in the air were making it hard for me to think coherently in any direction. After a moment, Jayne sighed and leaned back on her elbows again, and the number two gripper on her union-suit gave way under the strain with hardly a sound. The first one had been undone when she had emerged from her snow togs.

"We won't even dare mention that goddam proto-planet when we get back," she said in a low voice. "Not unless we can make a save on the satellite, and get ourselves back in the IGY's good graces. I'm on your side a hundred per cent now, Julian—I'm only sorry it took me so long."

"Glad to hear it. I hope it isn't too late."

"I really don't think it is. We've got to change Geoffrey's attitude somehow. Or if we can't, we've got to change the whole tack of the expedition—over his head if we can't manage it any other way."

Wentz stirred and coughed harshly, making my own lungs ache in sympathy. Jayne crossed her feet and got up, losing the gripper just over her navel in the process, and strode over to him, but he was asleep again. She knelt, her broad rear encased as tautly as a sausage, and took his pulse.

"How am I supposed to manage that?" I said thickly.

"I don't know," she said, coming back and sitting down beside me. "But it's got to be done somehow. I'm finally getting sick of the son of a bitch, Julian, I'll tell you that. I'm nothing to him when the chips are down. He doesn't even know I exist. I'm just a publicity-getting machine—until he's gotten where he wants to go, and then I'm not even good for that any more. I'm no use to him as a woman even at home; he just laughs at me. God knows I do everything I can, but if he notices, he just thinks it's funny. Once I tried to pay him off in Coquilhatville with our head bearer, just to see if he had any reactions left at all. Jesus, that was awful. I only meant to punish him, but I got more than I bargained for in the boy—it'd been a long time, anyhow. I suppose they heard me cooing all over the camp. Geoffrey laughed his fat head off."

She put her hand to her throat and just breathed for a moment, her breasts outlined under the absurd red cloth as though the suit had been sprayed on her. Then she said: "What I want to know is, what's in it for me? Sure, I get publicity too, and I won't pretend I don't lap it up. And it keeps me around him most of the time; what the hell, I still love him, I suppose, though I can't figure out what for any longer. But it isn't enough."

I was frozen to the spot. I knew what she was talking toward now, all right, and the fact that she seemed pathetic to me had melted the barrier of revulsion I had felt toward her phoniness and her fleshly extravagance.

It wouldn't take much to call forth from me the answer she was seeking. I tried to remember that it was only another bad means, and that with the Farnsworths even the ends seldom turned out to be worth much—but that only reminded me in turn that the situation might be even worse if I ducked, and that in any event I could hardly go on ducking for the rest of the summer without creating a real explosion. And there was Midge, too, a wavering, blurred image on another planet millions of years in the future. . . .

At the same instant, the pressure lamp's hissing sharpened suddenly and then quit, and with it went the light, obliterating everything. I felt Jayne move beside me, and then her hand just above my knee. In a last grasp at straws I tried to think of Harriet, but I could not even remember her name.

I went over like a tree, into a wriggling, smothering fury of arms, legs, breasts, and popping grippers. Her ample mouth found the angle of my jaw first, and then it was devouring mine, and she was forcing my hand down with hers. In the sudden darkness it was like being attacked unexpectedly by some completely unknown animal, shaggy and merciless——

Then came the sound, and I panicked completely. It was a long, jagged gasp, loud and inhuman, up in the middle of the stifling black air. I stiff-armed Jayne brutally back into the bedding and scrambled to my hands and knees, my arms trembling with strain.

"Jesus Christ, what was *that?*"

"Nothing! I don't care!" She clutched at my shoulders. "Julian, don't go away——"

It came again, louder and more awful than before. I

154

broke free and reeled toward the lantern, striking my forehead stunningly against its base. Somehow I found it and turned the valve up, and got a wooden match out of my pocket. The lamp lit with a sodden thump and I backed it down to a safe level with shaking fingers.

Wentz was writhing like a figure in slow motion, thumping at his breastbone with his closed fist. His face was a deep suffused violet. Jayne took one look and surged to her feet in a single smooth lunge, suddenly as oblivious as I was to her three-quarter nakedness.

We got a tube down his windpipe as fast as we could, and when we turned him over he projected almost a pint of blood-streaked phlegm on to the floor. But it wasn't good enough. What he needed was oxygen. But there was none, anywhere in camp. We held his head hopelessly, trying to make him cough again.

It was all over in less than five minutes.

Book Three

XI

Just before the war, if you can remember that far back, the Northern Lights made an excursion all the way down the east coast of the U.S. into New Jersey—an event unusual enough to make the evening news reports on the radio, and to send me and Midge piling out of our apartment (there were no kids then, and no Pelham house either) to look for them. We saw them, but for all the impression they made on us, they might just as well have stayed home: they resembled nothing but far-distant, uncertain anti-aircraft searchlights, far out-classed by the nearer ones being used to the south to attract customers to cut-rate clothing stores on the Jersey meadows. I was disgusted; Midge, who had expected nothing, only shrugged.

I never saw them again, for of course they're invisible even at the Pole in the summer. We buried Joe Wentz, instead, under a day magic to which no writer on the Arctic has ever bothered to give a name, though it is almost always visible if the sky is clear. It is also often visible from commercial airliners in any latitude, I have since discovered. That morning, I asked Elvers about it.

"Yes," he said. "Copper dawn. There is a legend about it. Tell you, some day."

The term was certainly odd, but I saw the justice in it. The effect is not really a dawn, for it can be seen at almost any time during the day, just as we saw it at the

Pole; but it looks like one. The sky must be blue and open, except for a few high feathers of ice-crystals; and the ground—"ground" in the painter's sense, whether it be a polar ice-field or an underlying layer of heavy cumulus at 9,000 feet—must be white, with hummocks of shadow. Then, on the horizon, you will see low-lying, tenuous clouds which glow like metal heated in a furnace. They are the high ice-feathers reflecting back to you the light of the sun overhead, making a false dawn, or a false sunset, in the very midst of daylight.

It had been our first intention to build Wentz a cairn, but Elvers advised against it. He could not guarantee, he said formally, that any cairn would be dog-proof, let alone bear-proof. The only alternative was to wrap the body in weighted canvas and bury it "at sea", through a hole cut in the ice. We cut one some distance from the camp, though actually its location made no difference whatsoever. We only felt that it did.

We gathered, the five of us . . . *my God, is five* that *much smaller a number than six?* . . . without any exact notion of how we were to proceed, or what to say to each other. Jayne and I stood as far apart as possible. Elvers brought the body, on a sledge pulled by five dogs led by the marten-masked face of Chinook; he and Farnsworth sawed out the hole in the ice. Then there was a long pause.

"I'd better say something, I suppose," Farnsworth said.

Nobody nodded. I at least felt that we were a long way from God. Farnsworth pushed his hood back and looked nervously at the black hole in the ice. Then, slowly, almost whispering at first, he said:

"This is Joseph Wentz, who came here with us to learn something more about the world he was born in. If there is a God and He's listening, He made this man. Through him He learned something new about Himself. Now we give Joe to His care, and we hope it will be better care than we gave him. We did not love him well enough, and we suspected that his Creator did not love him at all. We hope we were wrong."

Farnsworth paused and for a moment I thought he had finished; he was quite immobile. But then, his breath white around the rime-caked fur beside his mouth, he said:

"If You exist, God of the monobloc, and if You are still thinking about men, think of Joe Wentz. He admired Your fine workmanship in the stars, and never reproached You for spoiling him. We commit his body to Your ocean, in Your name. Amen."

Farnsworth lifted his head and nodded once to Elvers. The dog man, however, did not seem to get the signal; he was looking down at the body. For quite a long while we simply stood there, unwilling to speak, while the sun remained suspended in the blue sky, enswathed in brilliant haloes. Then, one by one, we began to stir and look resentfully at Elvers.

"There is no God," he said suddenly, in an empty, even voice. He had not even cleared his throat; he simply began to speak. Farnsworth took a step forward, but obviously he was as stunned as the rest of us.

"There is no God," Elvers said. "We know this, be-cause if there were a God, the Divine Hand would have fallen long ago, and made an end. There is only *das Unaufhoerliche;* it does not permit itself to be understood,

158

and its name is also unspeakable. Here is a man who died because he tried to speak it."

"This is no time for a course in German metaphysics." Farnsworth said harshly. "Do your job, Elvers. You're here to bury him."

"If a God made the monobloc, He is surprised and alarmed at what has come out of it," Elvers said, still looking at the ground. "He is an epicurean God, fleeing from what he has made; has been gone for aeons; cares nothing for His work; wants nothing but rest; has never heard of justice. It is proven: He never punishes crime; He cares nothing for stars; why should He care about men? Joseph Wentz is what we all are, a dog He has turned out into the streets to starve. This God has left us His whole world on our doorstep. *Bury it*, He said before He left, *before My other dogs shred it*. It is only fishheads and seal-blubber and carrion; bury it. And bay at the moon, if you like."

"Elvers," Klein said hoarsely, "if you don't shut up, I'll kill you where you stand."

Fred had spoken for me—I certainly could not have spoken for myself. Though I am not religious, I was sweating with fright as well as rage.

Elvers did not seem to hear; but with a quick, awkward surge of his back and shoulders and arms, he took hold of the horns of the sledge and heaved them up. The shrouded corpse lurched, slid board-rigid under the rumps of the two drawboard dogs, and went silently, feet first, into the hole in the ice. For a moment it seemed to want to float; then the canvas around the chest gave up a blurt of air, and in an instant Wentz was gone, like a child who had never even been born.

"Amen," Elvers said. He seemed to be subsiding inside his chafing-suit, like a melting wax statue; with Wentz gone, all the awful boldness of his speech was running down into his shoes and leaking out on to the ice; he looked, now, even more nondescript than he had looked the first time I had seen him. Fred Klein, who had been within an inch of smashing his teeth in, pulled back uncertainly.

"Down," Elvers said, looking up at Fred. "Down he goes. I meant no harm. Fred, I'm your friend. He's gone; I did my part. Didn't I?"

"You son of a bitch!"

"No, no, not me. He's gone. Down. *Au secours*, man-god. *Hjalpe*, god-dog. Go down and hide; end as a thing; that's how it goes. Please? Have I misunderstood? I didn't mean; he was dangerous. Please?"

"Elvers," Farnsworth said in a scalding whisper, "get out of here. I give you fifteen seconds."

Elvers straightened to attention like a model soldier. "Of course, Geoffrey," he said obediently. Then his whip cracked, making me start violently; the lash seemed to have issued straight out of his sleeve. Chinook bawled, and the other four dogs in the team lunged to their feet with snarls of alarm.

"Hi!" Elvers shouted. "Mush! Mush, you blubber-tubs! Gee! Gee! Mush!"

The sledge was dragged in a great half-circle and went away, picking up speed. Nobody moved until Elvers' cries to his dogs were almost drowned out by the wind. Then Fred Klein drew a long, shaky breath.

"Christ, Geoffrey," he said. "There's another man gone. What are we going to do now? Lock him up? We can't—we've got nothing to keep him in, and we can't spare anybody to mount guard on him."

"Besides," I said, "we need him to get back, when we're through."

"I can drive dogs," Geoffrey said grimly. "He's having a spell, that's all. I've seen it before."

"Never like this," Jayne said, her lips white. The Commodore didn't contradict her. Elvers was now out of sight in the glare, but his voice suddenly came blowing back over the contorted ice.

"Hip-ip-ip-ip! Ip-ip! Mush, mush! Hip-ip-ip! Ip hip-ip ipipip!"

This time, I was not so sure that he was laughing—but I knew well enough that I was going to be sick before I could tear my eyes away from that slowly-freezing well of oily black sea.

Camp life went on, however shakily. It could not have been stopped for more than a few hours without endangering the lives of everyone remaining, and it was harder work than ever now.

Both Fred and I joined to give Geoffrey a hand on the dredging, which was now about the only project—except for weather recording—that we had both the manpower and the skills to prosecute. Essentially we were using Farnsworth's coring rig, with the donkey-engine; but for the heavier loads brought up by the bucket, we had to mount the glass line. The stuff was very light in weight, despite the fact that it would outpull steel cable, which was what had made it possible for us to ship it in on the sleds; but it had come with us wound on a flat, so that unshipping the nylon line from the reel and rewinding the glass line was as tedious as carding wool.

Under those circumstances, it could hardly matter what I thought about Farnsworth's protoplanet, but I went right on thinking about it anyhow. As far as the outside world was concerned, I had decided to suppress the discovery until the evidence became absolutely over-whelming. On the surface, it was a reasonable decision, since I was sure anything less in the way of evidence would be useless, our credibility as scientific observers and reporters being now at its lowest possible ebb. I was painfully aware, all the same, that evidence that *I* would consider "overwhelming" would now have to be some-thing so spectacular as to be virtually beyond attaining —and that such an outcome would take me off the hook without my having to face the problem over again, except inside myself.

But whenever I thought of my future, I kept seeing instead a vision of Jaime Feliz, a one-time hero of science writing, and now one of the NASW's principal whipping-boys. After writing a book about chemical research called *Molecules and Their Masters* which became a best-seller, poor Jaime became so carried away by the taste of money that he fell into the clutches of MACB(eth), and was now touting anything he was told to tout in a syndi-cated column circulated throughout Latin America— not, of course, as a MACB(eth) staffer, but as an apparently independent science writer. ("Chemistry in Your Life, by the author of *Molecules and Their Masters*.")

Farnsworth and I worked outside for the most part, Fred inside; it was Fred's job to do every subtle thing he could to validate that sedimentary-rock meteorite before it was submitted to his colleagues back home, and it was ours to bring up another one by brute force, if we could.

It was this latter event that I was almost sure would not happen, and consequently—despite the constant spectre of Jaime Feliz—it became my test for "overwhelming evidence". I think, too, that I was hoping, without voicing the hope precisely to myself, that Fred's tests might so reduce the existing tiny sample as to make it a doubtful object for other geologists—or perhaps obliterate it altogether. Had I thought this wish out consciously, I would have known that it was idiotic, since I knew that Fred was too experienced a man to run any such risk. As it was, however, it remained in my mind as a vague, half-formed faith that the whole question would go away of itself if only I ignored it.

Almost nothing was said about Elvers. I could see that Geoffrey was worrying, but he simply would not talk. Somewhere behind his theatrically impassive face he was mulling over some theory while we worked over the winch, and it was sure to be a beaut when he finally let us know what it was, I was positive; but I could not draw him out; my first attempts at probing drew only abstracted scowls, and soon even these stopped appearing. I gave it up, for the time being.

But I could hardly stop thinking about it, especially since Elvers himself took to showing up while we were working, even on days when he was supposed to be out fishing (as he had to be pretty regularly now, to keep the dogs fed). There was something about the grappling operation that seemed to be drawing him toward it more and more often—though he never told us what it was, and Farnsworth didn't ask him; indeed Farnsworth gave a convincing imitation of a man who didn't know that Elvers was there. I knew he was there, all right. He doubled the amount of work I had to do, since I was obstinately determined never to turn my back on him no matter how many extra manœuvres that involved.

And, as it turned out, it was a good thing—from Farnsworth's point of view—that Elvers had become fascinated with the winch, and was there on the spot the Sunday that we hit the Lump. Otherwise, we would never have been able to get it free of the ocean bottom.

Not that the Lump turned out to be terribly heavy. Once we had cleaned it, it didn't quite make fifty pounds. All the same, it was a big piece of rock for our donkey-engine to handle. We had to wrench it out of a bed of gluey clay which resisted us with hundreds of foot-pounds of drag, and then pull it through layer after layer of overlying bottom soils, many of which stuck to it in thick gobbets all the way through its upward passage in the cold waters to the ice itself. Not even Elvers could have helped us to save it alone; during the last fifteen minutes of fighting that cold stone fish out into daylight, we had to call Fred out too. What we would have done had we needed a fifth pair of strong arms, I don't know.

Oh, I suppose we would have called Jayne, whom I knew to be quite as strong as I was; I doubt, however, that she could have gotten there in time. The crucial moment came when the grapples slipped, when—according to the pay-in marks on the cable—we had the Lump within fifteen feet of the surface. Geoffrey slipped the clutch, dropping line, and made another grab. He secured it—though he might just as easily have lost it for good—but the thump when the thing took up the slack again broke one of the poles of the rig. During the rest of the haul, we had to hold the rig rigid by hanging on to it with all our combined weights and with every dyne we could command from our exhausted muscles, making of ourselves human buttresses through which the snorting donkey-engine could pass its stubborn horses of drag.

The Lump came out into the air and we swung it on to the ice, where it lay oozing slow runnels and leaking a grey-brown stain, like the severed head of a great mud statue. I had never in my life seen anything less likely to launch a whole new era of knowledge. It had no shape, no particular colour, no special texture, no integrity as an object at all. It was just a large, heavy wet mark on a frozen white ground.

"Cripes," I said disgustedly, trying to wipe the sweat off my forehead before it froze to the lining of my hood. "That's the ugliest notion the Creator's had since the Surinam Toad. Let's chuck it back in."

"Why?" Fred Klein said. He didn't seem to be paying much attention, which I suppose was just as well.

"Oh, give any reason you like. Say it's out of season. Or that it's about to become a mother. Or that the question violates your right of free assembly."

"It's pretty big," Fred said slowly. "About four feet through, wouldn't you say? Obviously it can't be homogeneous, or it would have been even heavier. It must have a light core of considerable size."

He approached it cautiously, and sank the sharp rounded end of his spatula into its side. It cut like stiff cheese. In only a moment, the knife ground against some harder surface inside, and he began to cut laterally. As soon as he had cut himself a hand-hold, he was able to peel the rind of clays free of the inner surface, in long, cohesive strips. Underneath, there was rock: rough, dirty, disreputable-looking stuff, but inarguably rock.

"Graywacke," Fred said, almost inaudibly. "Almost a smooth ball of it, with a vitreous surface—you can hardly see the grains. And look: a flow-apron! It's been broken and most of it's been eaten away since, but it begins here—see—and there's enough left of the curve to re-construct it. This must have fallen relatively slowly, otherwise it would have exploded."

"Fred," I said, "what's graywacke?"

"Why, it's an aggregate, like sandstone, but much harder and finer-grained. When the grains and the paste are of the same mineral class, it's often difficult to tell graywacke from igneous rock without a microscope. This one looks like a mixture of quartz and porphyry, in a felspathic cement. I wonder if we'll find any ripple-marks? Rock of this kind on Earth came mostly from the Palaeozoic sea-beds. I don't quite see how it could be formed otherwise."

"Now wait," I said. "Do you mean that this is a meteorite? of *sea-formed* rock?"

"Well, it's certainly a meteorite," Fred said cautiously. "It can't very well have gotten where it was, and into the shape it's in, unless it fell from a standing start from a long distance. By the same token, 'from a standing start' is important; this thing wasn't part of any swarm, with an orbital velocity of its own. It started at infinity and fell straight down."

"How do you know?" Farnsworth said in a tight, intense voice.

"By the fact that it still exists," Fred said, looking a little surprised. "If it had been going any faster than

166

escape velocity when it hit the atmosphere, the heat would have exploded it into thousands of little pebbles, damn few of which would have hit the ground at all. Not even graywacke is compact enough to survive the velocity with which most meteors hit the air; you'll never find a meteorite of conglomerate, even presuming that any such meteors exist." He looked sidelong at the Lump. "And I'm beginning to believe that they do."

"How old is it?" Farnsworth demanded urgently.

"That depends on what you mean by old. Graywacke takes millions and millions of years to form. If you mean, how long has it been down under us, well—ten thousand years would be about the right order of magnitude, give or take a thousand. Certainly no longer that that; not even the clay capsule could have preserved the glazing any longer."

"Elvers," Farnsworth said, "go get a sledgehammer. There's one in the radio shack. And pick up a cold chisel and a mallet from the tool cache. We're going to split this thing open."

"Geoffrey, don't do that!" Fred said, watching Elvers scamper off with anxious eyes. "You'll spoil the configuration if you split it. And that's all we have to prove that it's a meteorite."

"Never mind," Farnsworth said grimly. He shoved the shorting flange on the donkey-engine up against the protruding spark-plug head with the toe of his boot; the engine died in mid-splutter. "It's got a vitrified surface, hasn't it? Let them explain that away. I want that damned Lump split. If it's a bottom-formed rock, I want to know about it right now. If there were seas on the protoplanet, and they lasted long enough to produce a rock this old,

167

then the planet must have been even bigger than anybody ever dreamed. And my God, Fred, if it was destroyed only ten thousand years ago—! That's almost within recorded history. We can't let *that* hang in doubt."

"I don't think you ought to split it," Fred said doggedly. "Let's get it back home and go at analysing it slowly. We'll need plenty of consultation, and fully equipped laboratories. This is no job for a sledgehammer, Geoffrey. Think what it is that you're doing."

"I know what I'm doing," Farnsworth said between white lips. "If that Lump has ripple-marks in it, I want to see them *now*. Elvers, give me that hammer. And stand back."

Farnsworth kicked aside the disintegrating peeled clay rinds, and set his feet solidly on the ice. As he slid one hand down to the head of the hammer, I knew at last what his keg-chested, long-legged frame had been trying to remind me of: that long-vanished, harbour-straddling wonder of the ancient world, the Colossus of Rhodes, toppled from its brass eminence by an earthquake more than two centuries before Christ at the age of fifty-six, and sold for scrap eight centuries later by the Saracens to the first man able to muster nine hundred camels to carry it away——

The hammer came down.

The Lump split with a crack as loud as a pistol shot, and collapsed on the ice into three rocking, irregular pieces. Farnsworth dropped the sledge and knelt. Fred, shrugging his shoulders, walked over to stand beside him, looking down fatalistically.

"Well?" Farnsworth said in a tight voice. "See anything?"

168

"Nothing much," Fred said slowly. "If there are ripple marks in there, the rock ought to have split in a flat plane—the ripples form on the surface of the ocean-bottom, so there ought to be a sharp division between the top of that layer and the bottom of the next. Of course, maybe you didn't hit it in the right spot."

"I'll hit it again. Where would you suggest?"

"I'd suggest leaving it alone," Fred said, with the first trace of asperity I had ever heard from him. "It's going to be of no use to you as a pile of rubble."

"It's no use to me as anything else if it's only a sedimentary meteorite," Farnsworth growled. "I've already got one of those. What's that squiggle there?"

His gloved finger traced over about an inch on one of the exposed faces. I couldn't see what it was; from where I was standing, it was masked by the rest of his hand.

"I don't know," Fred said. He got reluctantly down on his own knees. "It's a flaw of some sort. Maybe part of a dendrite, though they're anything but common in graywacke. Odd."

The geologist's hand groped about on the ice until it encountered the mallet. Farnsworth put the chisel into his other hand. He set the edged tool carefully and hit it a short, firm blow.

The fragment of the Lump parted again, this time in an even plane, as though Fred had knocked upon a door. He peered intently at the exposed surfaces, his nose only a few inches from the fresh rock.

"There are your ripple marks," he said at last, almost in a whisper. "But you can discount them now——"

"Discount them!" Farnsworth shouted, springing to his feet. "Great Jehosephat, Fred, we're going to rub every nose in the world in those ripple-marks! I *knew* we had to split that goddam Lump!"

"Listen to me, Geoffrey," Fred said, his voice even lower and more intense than before. "There's something here that's far more important than ripple-marks. Look here." He pointed. "Look closely. Do you know what those are?"

Farnsworth dropped down again and leaned over the rock. I still could not see what it was that they were looking at, but the expression of dawning, fanatical triumph on the Commodore's face was more than frightening enough. He said nothing for a long time; then, huskily:

"Fossils, Fred?"

"Yes," the geologist said. "Fossil crinoids. Two of them. And possibly two or three tentacles from a third."

I overcame my paralysis of alarm almost instantly. I don't even remember running over there; suddenly, I had my nose as close to that opened face of the Lump as either of them.

I am no geologist, but I've seen fossil crinoids before, they're hard to mistake. They look like miniature dust-mops with flexible handles. These were small, and one was imperfect. The intact one, too, was atypical, but the differences were not as great as I would have expected, considering where the Lump had come from. When you thought about that gap of millions upon millions of miles of dark vacuum, what was surprising was how much the fossil *resembled* Palaeozoic types evolved on the Earth.

Farnsworth had made it. The asteroidal protoplanet was a fact—complete with "evidences of life".

XII

The first one to break the silence was Elvers, who said:
"That reminds me, Julian. I promised to tell you the legend about the copper dawn."

"Not now, for heaven's sake. This is no time for that. Geoffrey, if——"

"It's one of the oldest legends we have," Elvers said. "People say that in the time before the war there was much more air to breathe than there is now, and it was warmer most of the year, even at night. But as a result of the weapon we used against Nferetet, we lost a lot of that air. That brought the ice-crystal cloud layer down to within sixty miles of the ground. Since then we see the copper dawn almost every day, except during sandstorms, of course."

Farnsworth stood up and looked toward the radio igloo, shading his eyes with his hand. "He's out of his mind," he said with abstracted irritation. "Jayne's coming this way. That's timing it neatly, I must say."

I was watching Elvers closely now. He didn't sound much crazier than he had before, which had been quite crazy enough to suit me; but he was plainly in a terrible state of the trembles. Something seemed to have frightened him profoundly—and what could it have been but the Lump? Why that should be I could only dimly guess, but he was the only one of the four of us who had yet to move a step closer to it, let alone touch it. Even his face was turned away; he was looking at the horizon, though there was no copper dawn visible now.

"Is that all there is to it, Elvers?" I said.

"That's all there needs to be," Elvers said in a sing-song voice. "It's the brand on our brows. It reminds us of all the blood we shed. No, that isn't all. It reminds us that we will yet have to wade in more blood, to keep the secret."

Under those conditions I would have thought it impossible to feel a chill, but I did. "I see," I said cautiously. "Is that what the voices say?"

He turned and looked at me blankly. "What voices?" he said. "It's only a legend. And a warning. That's all."

That was far from enough, but I had no chance to draw him out further, for Jayne was topping the nearest hummock and sliding down toward us.

"You're just in time," Geoffrey said. "We've got it, Jayne. We're made. Come take a look."

"In a minute. Listen, I've got news, and I couldn't get it all written out fast enough, there was so much of it. I've got to tell you right now before I garble it." She turned to me with a beaming smile. "Julian, Joe Wentz has been vindicated by your IGY friends—or forgiven, anyhow. It seems that he wasn't the first man to lose the satellite. He was probably the last man to see it, instead. They backtracked his figures, and it seems that his object came into sight at just the proper place and at the proper velocity, and that it changed course while he was watching it. None of the other observing teams have picked up a trace of it anywhere, and I gather that they've really combed the skies for it. I couldn't get all the details, but the essence of it is that it's vanished, just as though somebody's stolen it right out of the sky."

Abruptly, Elvers began to giggle. Jayne swung a furious, astonished glance on him. Without a moment's hesitation, he ran, scuttling over the hillocks toward the kennels.

"I loathe that crazy little bastard," Jayne said, staring after him. "Anyhow, they're still searching, and hoping to pin down the accident or whatever it was. They say it couldn't have changed course by itself and that the reasons why it did are probably very important. They say they want us to help, and they'll reinstate us in return for the favour. In short, complete capitulation! The question is, where do we take it from here?"

That wasn't the question in my mind. Mine was: *Who* had taken it from there? Staring down at that meteoric fossil, I was already beginning to wonder crazily whether or not I already knew the answer—and if I did, to whom in all the world I could possibly tell it.

I looked over at Farnsworth. His expression made it perfectly clear that he had been following much the same line of thought. It was a mixture of stunned triumph and genuine alarm.

"This would be funny, if it weren't so likely to be deadly," he said. "Jayne, you'd better come and take a look at the Lump here, so you'll know just what we're up against."

She walked around the grappling rig and looked down curiously while Farnsworth and Fred took turns explaining, and I stamped my feet. The rest of me was warm, thanks to the high reflectivity of the ice, but my boots knew I was at the North Pole. So did the end of my nose, despite the rabbit-skin patch on it.

"I think this is great," Jayne said. "But I don't see the connection."

"You tell her, Julian. Maybe she'll believe it, coming from you."

That startled me. I couldn't help wondering exactly what, other than self-knowledge, lay behind his putting it that way, but I could read nothing into his tone but the same grudging humility that the words seemed to be conveying. It seemed unlikely to me that Jayne would have told him what Joe's death had surprised us at. While it is true that hell hath no fury, etc., she hadn't exactly been scorned, either. I put my initial split-second inference down to pure jumpiness.

"We're in trouble with that wild-eyed guess Geoffrey was broadcasting back in the States, until Harriet made him stop it," I told Jayne. "The War Between Mars and the Asteroids. The science writers themselves never fell for it, but feature desks and columnists love anything that smacks of the fantastic. Just think back to the play they gave to the flying saucer stuff and you'll see what I mean."

"I still don't get it," Jayne confessed.

"All right, just add up the facts as they stand now. The satellite has vanished, nobody knows why. We have evidence here that shows there *was* once a large planet, with life on it, between Mars and Jupiter. What happens if we report that evidence now? The silly-season beat will consider the source, dig into the morgue, and the War Between Mars and the Asteroids will be revived instanter. Half the columnists in the country will call us fools and charlatans and publicity-grabbers—and the other half will be hinting darkly that the satellite was stolen by Martians."

Across the ice, I could see Elvers creeping back, and I wondered who we'd get this time—the trembling paranoid or the humdrum little albino chiropodist. This time he wasn't running, but as a datum that wasn't very illuminating.

"It's an irresistible hypothesis to the kind of brain that goes in for *Flabbergasting Stories*—or for Frank Scully and Gray Barker and Jessup and Adamski," I added. "It's got our boy Elvers, right now."

"Is *that* what all that rambling was about?" the Commodore said, startled. "I wasn't paying very close attention."

"I wasn't either, at first. But the point is this: we've got to decide whether or not we want to take the risk of letting that idea get into general circulation. The responsibility's entirely ours, and whichever decision we make may be the wrong one."

"Why do we need to bring the matter up at all?" Fred said.

"Fred, it isn't a question of our bringing it up. Geoffrey brought it up *in posse* months ago. They'll think he's trying to bring it up again, as soon as they get our report on the Lump, and then the business about the satellite having been stolen will follow naturally. There's where the danger lies."

"Why?" Fred said, more puzzled than ever.

"Well, first, because it might very well trigger a mass psychosis. The world's ripe for one. But, more important, because *there may be a small possibility that it's true*."

Fred looked stunned, Jayne angry; Farnsworth only nodded soberly.

"Look at it this way, Fred," the Commodore said. "That explanation has already been laughed at by the press, and it would be twice as funny coming from us now, even if we only imply it, by reporting what we've found. If it *does* turn out to be true, it will probably also turn out to have been very expensive to have laughed it off. Do we want to take that chance—tiny though I admit it is?"

"I think there's no such chance at all," Fred said. "But just for the sake of argument—well, if theft *is* the explanation, maybe it would be vital to get it on the air and get it circulating, whether people laugh at it initially or not."

"There's that," I admitted. "And that's why I say that no matter which way you look at it, the responsibility's ours. I can't think of any group in the world less competent to handle it, but that's academic now. It's in our hands, and there's nobody else we can shift it to."

Elvers giggled behind me. I jumped as though I had been stabbed. Some time during the course of the argument he evidently had made a wide half-circle on the ice, and had managed to come up behind all of our backs, or at least out of all of our fields of view. We were accustomed to ignoring him, anyhow. I whirled around in a hurry, coming within an ace of falling down.

He had his Parkchester with him, the special magazine-loading model they had given us to shoot polar bears and Russians with. Somehow I didn't doubt that he had kept it well oiled, unlike mine, with the special low-temperature silicones. It was pointed straight at

Farnsworth. Elvers' hands were trembling, but his aim did not vary enough at point-blank range for the trembling to make any difference.

"I am taking responsibility," he said, his teeth chattering so hard that it was almost impossible to understand him. I remembered that he had never seemed to be bothered by the cold.

"Elvers," Geoffrey said in a voice like the rumble of a tank, "drop that thing where you stand and go back to the kennels. If I have to take it away from you, I won't be gentle."

In that same voice, Geoffrey must at one time or another quelled whole rebellions, even in the middle of jungles and without any other weapon. You had only to hear it to believe that implicitly.

But it had no visible effect on Elvers. "You, Fred," he said. "Roll those four rocks back down the hole in the ice."

Fred's eyebrows went up for a moment. Then he grinned at Farnsworth's suddenly anguished expression.

"I don't want to do that," the geologist said gently. "Neither do you, Elvers—not after you worked so hard, helping us to bring them up. You're pretty sick. Better give me the gun, and we'll see if some rest will help."

"No," Elvers said between trembling jaws. "Roll those rocks into the water."

Fred shrugged. "Roll 'em yourself," he said.

The rifle swerved and went off. Almost instantly, it was boring straight at Geoffrey again.

A rifle designed to stop a quarter-ton polar bear is no weapon to use on a man at point-blank or any other range. Fred Klein, wearing an expression of infinite surprise, jack-knifed and toppled. Elvers had shot him through the heart with the precision of a master anatomist, but the high-velocity bullet had crushed his whole chest.

Every muscle in Farnsworth's big, clumsy body was as tight as a drum-cord, but Elvers never took his eyes off his boss; he knew who was dangerous and who wasn't. I was so sick I could hardly stand, let alone act.

"Jayne," Elvers said. He was chittering like a terrified squirrel. "Those rocks. Down the hole."

Jayne looked at her husband. The silence could not have been long, but it was the longest I have ever endured. Those pieces of the Lump were a summary of Geoffrey's whole life as an explorer, and of the reasons why he had very little life as anything else. He could, had he wanted to, have given Jayne's life for them; she would have allowed it, and he knew it; he needed only to tell her to stand fast. Or he might have given his own, by telling her to obey, and then charging Elvers; he just might have borne the crazy chiropodist down by sheer momentum even in dying. I am not sure how much good I would have been had he tried it, but I think I would have tried hard—and he must have known that he could trust Jayne in any free-for-all. And of course, he could have told her to obey, and done nothing, in the hope of exchanging the Lump for all of our lives, and for the shadow of another chance to take the responsibility that Elvers had pre-empted.

But in fact he did none of these things. He only stood, his face a huge mask of anguish. He looked utterly paralysed.

As that long second ended, Jayne turned her hooded head toward me. There was an anguish in her face, too, but there was no longer any doubt. Her eyes were half closed, and the look that she gave me through her pain was one of such raw sexual complicity that no other man could have failed to be aware of it.

But Geoffrey was not. He did not seem to be seeing anything. Jayne walked slowly to the four pieces of the Lump, swinging her hips, and knelt deliberately, offering me her rear like a cat in heat. At that moment I wouldn't have given a rouble and a half for Geoffrey Farnsworth, or any other husband in the world.

It took her a while to get the first piece of rock loose from the ice. At last, however, it rumbled to the lip of the hole and dropped, with a noisy splash. Jayne began to chip at the base of the second chunk.

"Not that one," Elvers said, gritting his teeth. "The other. With the fossils. You're saving it till last. Do it now."

I cleared my throat hoarsely, and his eyes darted briefly toward me. "I—I'd better help," I said.

"No. Not you. You're going home."

Jayne dropped the chisel and pushed. The rock with the crinoids in it bumped away from her thrusting hands, hesitated at the brink, and vanished into the black water. She straightened from her crouch, and, still kneeling, put her hands in the small of her back.

"I can't get the third piece through there," she said. "All the spray from the first two closed up the hole. It was half frozen already. You'll have to cut another."

Elvers craned his neck, but from where he was standing it was obviously impossible for him to see whether or not what Jayne had said was true. It sounded very likely to me, and perhaps it did to him. To make sure of it, however, he would have had to walk crabwise at least twenty paces, and risk losing his clear shots at one or another of us several times because of the rig in the middle. His eyes still glued to the Commodore, he said:

"Leave the other pieces there. Get up. All of you spread out in front of me. Turn your backs."

Jayne got to her feet. I managed to walk on my rubber legs until I was abreast of her.

"You too, Geoffrey. All three of you abreast. And stay that way. If you break rank, I'll shoot."

"Where to?" I said around the block of ice in my throat.

"The dog igloo."

I took a hesitant step forward and then stopped. I could still just barely see both the Farnsworths out of opposite corners of my eyes. Neither of them had moved. Geoffrey seemed almost hypnotized.

"MUSH!" Elvers screamed.

We stepped out. Behind our naked backs, Elvers giggled with soft appreciation.

It was a long scramble, since it had to be done as a march, though singly any one of us could have done it in fifteen minutes. I kept looking for a chance to throw myself down the opposite side of a crest and roll out of the line of fire, or for Jayne or Geoffrey to try it; but each time I saw such an opportunity, I realized that Elvers would shoot Geoffrey first in any case—and the moment's hesitation was enough. Before we had covered half the ground, I was praying that none of us should slip, let alone try to break free.

We were still three abreast when we came down the

boundary ridge of the large floe where Elvers had built his kennels, and began to sidle cautiously through a field of staked-out, snarling dogs.

Somehow I had not remembered that we had brought so many. Their shaggy heads began to strain up from the surface of the ice as soon as we began to walk from the rim toward the kennel. Inside the walls of the floe, the whole ice-floor seemed evenly dotted with those dishevelled, masked animal faces, rising from sprawled bodies so powdered over with snow as to look half sunken in the ice itself. Those we passed closest-to burst up grinning and yelping at the ends of their short tethers, and were answered by ragged cries from all through the eternally frozen, cobalt-domed hollow.

Even I could see without doubt that none of them had been fed in a long time, and had been brooding over their hunger in the ice until they had forgotten everything else. One poor beast that I skirted did not get up to snarl at me; he had somehow broken a hind leg, and was gnawing with horrible deliberation at his own gangrenous flank. The animals staked out nearest him were watching him with jealous, straining earnestness, their muzzles half-buried between their buried paws, only their black eyes and noses showing. When at Elvers' order we filed one by one, on our hands and knees, into their igloo, the whole floe behind us began to howl with their savage woe.

"This is our chance," Jayne whispered under the howling. "He's got to come down that tunnel himself. I'll kick him in the eyes from this side. You can kick the rifle out of his hands. Geoffrey, for God's sake get your carcass out of line with the tunnel. Julian?"

"Sure," I said shakily. We waited.

But Elvers did not come for several minutes. Finally, after the muted howling had died back a little, we heard a scrambling in the tunnel. I tried to lift my foot and keep my balance.

A dog came out of that tunnel as though it had been fired from a circus cannon. Neither of us even came close to catching it with a kick. It was going straight for Geoffrey, but we had no time to watch it. Another was already in the igloo, circling around the walls toward me; and another, and still another. Jayne was screaming. She had never told me that she was afraid of the dogs, and it was too late now. I went down, grabbing blindly, and caught the one that had hit me by the ears. His breath stank of fish and desperation. Teeth came down on my boot at the ankle, and ground the bones together——

A whip-end came out of the boiling air and took the dog whose head I was mauling off my chest, with a tremendous jerk. I grabbed instinctively at my foot, but my aim was bad; while I was still trying to get my gloves around the oily neckfur, the whip sounded in the igloo like the crack of judgment.

I still have no idea how Elvers managed to crack so long a lash inside that igloo, oversize though it was; you need lots of room to bring the tip of a whip past the speed of sound. But at the crack, however he managed it, the dogs flinched and dodged away from all of us. One of them—the one Elvers had snatched free of my hands with the whip—was huddled halfway across the floor, its back broken.

But the other three left it alone. They slunk on their

bellies into a huddle, as close to the tunnel as they thought the whip would allow them, and as far away from the corpse. There they crouched panting, flank to flank, their tongues out and dripping, like a litter of pups in high July.

Farnsworth rolled over and sat up, blowing the snow out of his nose and mouth. In the dim light it was hard to tell whether or not he had been hurt; he was breathing in convulsive snorts, but at least he seemed to be conscious. Jayne was leaning against the wall and sobbing, with her hands pressed to her face. I prodded my ankle cautiously, trying to discover whether or not my boot had been bitten through where the pain was. It had; there was blood leaking down inside it around my foot.

Elvers squatted down on his haunches beside the quivering dogs, holding his rifle more easily than he had before. He was still aiming it squarely at Geoffrey.

"Be careful of the dogs," he said. "They mind me. They won't mind you. If you try to rush me, you might make it. But none of us would live through it. These are close quarters—and you shouldn't excite the dogs outside. They're not securely tethered."

"You're a crazy damned slob of a murderer," Farnsworth whispered. "I'm going to kill you, Elvers."

"No," Elvers said, almost regretfully. "I'm not that crazy, Geoffrey. And I'm not a man at all, not in your sense. I'm a Martian. I find it hard to remember sometimes. We're all of us a little mad, but we're not men. I mean all of the people like me—not like you, Geoffrey. You're not a mad Martian, you're just a crazy man. I hope you see the difference."

Geoffrey said nothing. After a moment's wait, Elvers added:

"And that's why you're not going to kill me. No Earthman could. The Nferetetans tried hard while you were all still in caves, and even then they were more powerful than you are now. But we killed them instead. Understand, I don't want to have to kill you. You forced it on me. It's your own fault. I want you to understand that. We don't like to kill people. We're so tired of wading in blood, so tired of drinking blood, so tired of dreaming about blood——"

His voice went scooping up into the falsetto. The dogs yelled and scrambled to their feet, but the whip-lash came flicking out of his sleeve—I was now certain, even in this dim green-white light, that he really did keep it coiled up there—and they cowered back again after a moment's grim dance. The answering howl outside the igloo, however, rose and rose, like snowflakes picked up by a twister, flowering into an echoing fountain of savage dolor and falling drop by drop, petal by petal, back down on the whole Polar Basin. You have never known a countryside until you have heard it howl.

The dogs were sitting against him now, one on one side, two on the other, like broken wings in the dimness. I could think of nothing but Elvers' five words back beside the hole: *Not you. You're going home.* In the igloo they were not a promise, but a judgment and a sentence.

"I didn't tell you the whole legend," Elvers said, in a normal conversational tone. "Actually it's history, but only oral history. It may have been written down at one time, but of course all those records were destroyed. You see, not so long ago, about fifteen thousand of your years, there were two planets where the asteroid belt is now. One of them, Nferetet, was larger than the Earth, and had a moon nearly four hundred and eighty miles in diameter. The other one, Infteret, was two thousand miles through, about the size of your Moon. There was no life on Infteret; but on Nferetet we could see great seas, and vegetation. And in due course we could see lights at night there.

"And on one night we also saw lights on Infteret, and we knew that the Nferetetans had crossed the distance between them. This was something that we had known how to do long before, but we had found nothing interesting and the art had declined from disuse. And so we asked ourselves questions, because we knew that the Nferetetans would soon be crossing to our world.

"It was known that Nferetet and Infteret were doomed, because their orbits were perturbed by Fgath—Jupiter. And so some among us said, wait, and they will die by the hands of the gods. And others said, strike now, for the Nferetetans will seek to escape destruction by overrunning us. So because it was a little thing to move Infteret a little out of the way in its orbit, and a great thing to wait perhaps a million years more for Fgath to do it, we moved Infteret with an art we knew; and in a year it collided with Nferetet, and the lights went out, and both were shattered. And through this feat we also threw great quantities of our own air into space, and many of us died also.

"But we knew that there is life in many places, and that some day someone might come from some star who would be more powerful than we; and so we took up crossing space again, and found a small colony of man-like beings under a dome on Nferetet's moon, which still survived; and we destroyed the dome; and also all other evidences. And some day the asteroids themselves will be gone, and then the thing that we did will finally cease to exist, and we will never have done it at all."

"And is this," I said hoarsely, "all that you've been thinking about for fifteen thousand years? Just hiding a crime? What else have you been doing?"

"Nothing," Elvers said. "What else was there to do?"

"Bringing your own planet back to life. What are the canals for, if they're not for that?"

"There are no canals," Elvers said. "The marks you see are volcanic faults, left behind by the catastrophe, when we used the great force against Nferetet. We could bring our world back to life if we wanted to. But first there is the evidence."

"How does this affect us?" Jayne said in a low voice.

"We thought we were in control," Elvers said. "We knew you were learning spaceflight, and we had marked the day on our calendar. We were ready to discourage you. We stole your satellite, as a beginning.

"But what Geoffrey has done was beyond all prediction. When I heard what he was looking for, my friends and I made every effort to keep him from the Pole, but he was stubborn, and we could not show our hands too far. Very well, I said, he is a fool; let him go. He will only fall over his own feet and kill himself. And if he somehow survives, he will find nothing under that ocean but mud. Yet somehow he has survived, and he has found evidence of the crime. We had thought evidence of that kind existed only in the asteroid belt, and we meant to prevent your ever getting there. But Geoffrey found otherwise, and so all must die but Julian."

"Why not me?"

"You will go back and tell everyone that the expedition found nothing."

"And what about you?" I said.

"I will stay here," Elvers said. "My friends will take me off. It is quite comfortable here—for me."

XIII

However I looked at it, I knew I had heard my own death-sentence as well. It did not really matter whether or not I believed a word of what Elvers had said. He had a System. I might have raised all kinds of objections to it, but that would have been a sterile exercise even had I had the time and the courage. Whether I believed it literally or not, it was logical and self-consistent for Elvers, it fitted some of the facts, it provided some of the answers—and above all, he was committed to it. It would have been impossible to talk to him on any other grounds; the objective truth or falsity of the System was almost wholly beside the point.

In the world inside Elvers' skull, then, it was obvious that his "Martians" had changed in fifteen thousand years. They were not criminals now, though they still thought of themselves as criminals. They had become fanatical moralists. I didn't think it would be consistent with this character for them to compound their ancient crime by wiping out the life of still another planet, even to conceal the murder of the first one. (People in the fantasies of madmen are always more self-consistent and logical than real human beings; but then, if this was *not* just a fantasy, the people involved weren't human beings, either.) But Elvers was perfectly capable of completing the slaughter of the expedition, if he thought it would do any good. We had Fred Klein's perfectly real corpse as evidence for that.

"Elvers," I said, "your friends won't pick you up. They won't look kindly on your failure."

"Failure? I shan't fail, Julian." For a moment I thought he was smiling.

"You've already failed. I half suspected that you were going for your gun, when you ran away from Jayne. Just to be safe, I got the report about the Lump out on the air while you were gone. I wish I'd told you that then—it might have saved Fred's life."

"That is not true," Elvers said tonelessly. "That is not true."

Jayne cleared her throat. "It's true," she said. "I saw Julian run to the shack."

"Thanks, Jayne. So if you kill us all now—and you'll have to, because I'm not going back without these people—that report will remain hanging in the air. It will become one of the great questions of the International Geophysical Year. You know what'll happen then. Sooner or later, there'll be a huge force up here, dragging the Arctic Ocean from one side to the other for more meteorites."

"They will find none," Elvers said. But he said it almost like a question.

"You know they will. Look how quickly and easily we found the Lump. The bottom must be littered with them."

"Never mind," Elvers said. "You will deny all this."

"In a pig's ear I will. I'm staying here; I won't be home to deny it."

"You won't stay, Julian," Elvers said. "You're a

reasonable man. You have no stake in Geoffrey's expedition, or his protoplanet. You won't want to die for it."

"The protoplanet has nothing to do with it," I told him. "You know nothing about me, Elvers. I knew nothing about myself, as little as a month ago. You'd better strike a bargain with me."

"We never bargain," Elvers said simply.

"You'd better be glad I'm giving you the chance, this time. It's in your interest. If you let us live—all three of us—we'll take the hounds off your trail for good. We *will* forget the protoplanet."

Farnsworth looked up sharply at this, but I ploughed ahead. "When we get back home, we'll 'admit' that our original report was incorrect. In fact, we'll say that it was a deliberate fraud. You know what the people back home think of this expedition already. They'll believe an admission of fraud on sight. And then your friends can put their plans for keeping men out of space right back on the original schedule."

"You are tricking me," Elvers said, scowling. "You have a reputation to protect. You will never admit to such a fraud. And Geoffrey would be unable to keep any such promise."

At least he was arguing with me; it was a small enough sign, but a good one as far as it went. If he was as human as he looked, the notion of leaving three people alive who knew his power and his triumph would be hard to resist. If he was not human, of course, I had no criteria to go by at all.

"Whatever Geoffrey says won't matter, if *I* say it was a fraud," I said.

"But why would you do that?"

"Because I think we'll win in the long run," I said. "I think your people have gone frozen in the brains. No matter how powerful they are, they've stopped growing; they haven't thought a single new thought in fifteen thousand years, by your own testimony. That isn't true of the human race. The human mind is still unfrozen. We've only just barely tapped it. I've got the utmost confidence in our ability to out-think you people six ways from Sunday, in any long-term competition. But I *don't* want to see the two races clash head-on now, while your people are millennia ahead of us technologically. We'll catch up in due course. Right now, I'm going to keep your secret, for the benefit of my own race—even if it does make me an accessory to your mass murder."

I was caught up in the thing myself by the time I finished speaking. For those few moments, I really believed in those Martians and Nfertetans. Perhaps it was just as well. Madmen are intensely suspicious of being humoured, and intensely sensitive to play-acting.

He started to speak, hesitated, and for the very first time turned his head to look directly into my face.

That was what I had been praying for all along, but I almost lost the opportunity; the shock of looking into those eyes was paralysing. Yet somehow I got out of my squat and dove headlong for his belly.

He squealed like a pig. The gun went off with a blast like the breaching of a fortress. I took it full in the face and was instantly blind and deaf. All I could do in the roaring blackness was to hang on, butting and kicking and using my weight as best I could. Even my sense of balance was gone. I was conscious only of blows being rained all over me, and my strength and my breath running out of me. Finally somebody caught me by the hair and threw me back on the ground. It knocked the wind out of me. All I could do was double up and gasp.

For long ages, nothing else happened at all inside my limited consciousness; I was utterly cut off from the world outside my own wretched skin. Then the roaring in my ears began to subside, and I could hear someone sobbing, far off in the distance. At first, I thought it was myself.

"Julian. Julian."

I moaned and tried to sit up. I didn't make it.

"Julian. Wait a minute."

"Jayne?"

"Yes. My God. Are you hurt?"

"I don't know. I can't see. What happened?"

She sobbed again. "Geoffrey's. . . . Elvers clubbed him with the gun. He's d-dead."

"Elvers is dead?"

"Yes, him too. The dogs. . . . My God."

"But how did Elvers——?"

I was hearing better, but not seeing at all, and my eyes were beginning to burn. I touched my face tentatively. There did not seem to be any blood.

"He . . . didn't hit Geoffrey when he fired. Geoffrey jumped him too. So did I. But my God, Julian—he stood up with all of us on top of him. He swung the gun and. . . . It was the dogs. They turned on him. I got the gun away from him and hit him on the head and he went down and the dogs came pouring in and—Julian, Julian, my God, *they ate him*——"

I put out my hand to her, and, by accident, found her. I held on until her sobs began to subside slightly.

"He had it coming," I said. "Can you help me up? I've got a bad foot. And I—think there's gunpowder in my eyes."

After a moment, I felt her arm under my shoulders. She helped me gently to a sitting position.

"Julian," she said. "Why did you do it?"

"I knew he wouldn't shoot me," I said, dabbing at my burning cheeks. "He had to leave somebody alive. If he'd been going to kill us all, he wouldn't have bothered to tell us his crazy story."

No, that was no good; I still couldn't see. I tried to wash my eyes with snow.

"So he picked me," I said, wincing. "But he had the gun on Geoffrey. I had to jump him to give Geoffrey a chance. I thought it would spoil his aim. I—I'm sorry it wasn't enough. He didn't look so strong."

The snow didn't work, either. I got painfully to my hands and knees.

"I know what you did it for," Jayne said quietly. "But you still didn't say why you did it."

I felt her hand. She guided me to the entrance tunnel and I crawled. After a while, I began to see a little, but only a dim wash of light, without any definition. I lifted my head; since I didn't bump it, I straightened up. In a moment she was outside beside me and was helping me to stand.

"I don't know," I said. A line came out of my memory, and without thinking, I said it: "*E se tu mai nel dolce mondo reggi.*"

She sighed. "I don't know what that means," she said.

"You'd better lean on me, Julian. It's uphill from here for a while."

I began to limp along beside her. I'd been about to say, *Nobody knows what that means*; but suddenly, I wasn't sure it was true.

My hearing came back. My eyesight did not improve at all, and the pain got steadily worse.

Jayne helped me to stump about the silent ruins, bound my ankle, tried to treat my eyes. She did not want me to walk, but I had to. We were hardly able to speak; but then, there was nothing to say. The débâcle had spared nothing.

Chinook had been killed in the last struggle—whether by Elvers or not we could not decide. Most of the other dogs who had broken free, as Elvers had known they would, to join the carnage in the igloo, were either dead or wounded beyond salvation. Those that had not been hurt were too starved even to howl any longer, and we could not feed them. I was glad I could not look into their eyes. Long ago I would have claimed that their suffering was not my fault.

Now I knew that all suffering was my fault. The personal devil is not a joke. If you believe in him long enough, he will open your eyes. God doesn't dare.

Jayne led me to the last remaining parts of the Lump, and under my direction we destroyed them, with thermit. The intense blue-white light was almost cheerful; while it lasted, I could even see Jayne, as a sort of candle-flame made of shadow. She looked impossibly graceful, and the heat of the thermit bomb struck deeply into my bones, like a blessing. As for the Lump, the ice under it did not melt even under that ardour, but I was satisfied; no eye would ever make sense of the puddle of slag that we left there. Geoffrey's pebbles and tektites we simply threw out into the snow. When we were through, we had emptied both Geoffrey and Elvers of any meaning their deaths might have conferred upon their lives.

Then we called for help. I didn't try to talk to Harry Chain; by then I was in a white universe of pain almost ecstatic in its purity. I heard his voice, and then Jayne's, and then, I think, Harriet's voice sobbing hysterically. After that, Jayne and I bedded down together in the radio shack.

Perhaps we made love. I don't remember. I would like to think that we did.

The planes came for us in the "morning". Word had been going out all night long on the air, warning of a rescue mission, and threatening war and worse if anyone interfered with it. We could have heard that, had we been awake and listening for anything so trivial. But we knew nothing about it until we heard the planes arriving —a huge Paisecki helicopter with a fighter escort—and staggered out.

The air was full of whirling and roaring. I was taken by both arms; somebody else thumped me on the back, I suppose to encourage me, or maybe even to congratulate me.

"Jayne! Jayne!"

I heard her voice somewhere, but the noise drowned out the words. I was propelled gently up a cleated ramp.

But they did not take off right away. As I found later, they loaded everything that remained: all the torn tents, all the live dogs, the useless apparatus, the sleds, the records, the guns, the trash . . .

. . . and alas, the frozen bodies of Geoffrey and Fred. We had not done with climbing that mountain yet.

Book Four

XIV

I am not going to talk about anything else that is on the public record. That would be senseless. If you like to go to trials, the newspapers and the magazines and the transcripts remain for you to read.

They won't tell you, for instance, about the first thing that I saw after I was taken off the Pole. The doctor on the whirly-bird looked at my face and said, "Jesus Christ", and from there on I was in isolation for many weeks. Evidently he knew exactly what it was that he was seeing, and told the radioman, and the radioman told Alert; and so they held us all up—not just me—in Alert, while they worked to get the gunpowder out of my festering eyes.

During all that time I spoke to nobody but doctors and orderlies, all of whom either did not know the answers to my questions, or would not tell me. Of course, sometimes I asked the wrong questions. Once while the pain after the operation was becoming distracting again, I asked my surgeon, "Where are the kids?" I meant Harry Chain and Harriet, and perhaps he would have told me if I'd been able to put it more sensibly; he surely knew that both of them were right there on the base. But the poor booby thought I meant my own children, and he said they were fine, just fine, and I'd . . . see them in a little while; and of course I forgot Harriet instantly and wept, which upset him terribly. I was not supposed to weep for at least a week yet; it was bad for my eyes.

But I couldn't blame him. He was more interested in those grains of gunpowder. If I'd told him that I hadn't wept for twenty-five years, and that if I waited to weep one more day I would dry up for ever, he would have thought I was crazy.

And to give them credit, when the bandages came off I really did see pretty well. Things were a little foggy, that's all, and I'm used to that. Any man who has worn glasses since childhood knows that the world goes foggy when he takes them off, and comes to think of the world as a naturally foggy place. When he finds that the glasses don't disperse the fog, he shouldn't be greatly surprised.

It was the habit of seeing that gave me more trouble. For several days I saw, but I couldn't interpret what I saw. The doctors and orderlies helped me, most patiently, out of my initial despair. Much sooner than I had hoped, I began to be able to turn all those blobby geometries into nurses and doctors and orderlies and ward-boys and walls and floors and all the rest.

The fact that nearly everything was white helped. I had been used to that, just before Elvers pulled his trigger, and still my strongest, most recent memory of sight was that of looking for the outlines of things in a white world where colours did not code, but only decorated.

With procaine in my eyes to ease the burning, they let me walk up and down corridors where there was nothing special to see, and then they tried me in rooms with pieces of static meaninglessly-placed furniture. I did well. By this time I was able to ask coherently after Harriet and Jayne and Harry, and was told that they were all right here with me on Ellesmere—which was the first time I had been told where I was.

You mean I'm still in Alert?

Yes—they said—at the base hospital.

But where's the wind?

Oh, you can't hear the wind here—indulgently— we're far underground. Now, Mr. Cole, how many fingers am I holding up?

Several. My God. When can I go home?

In a while. But *exactly* how many fingers?

That depends. How many pies do you need fingers for?

(Better let him rest a bit.)

It went on like that. Once in that wilderness which I could no longer hear howling, they brought in a mass of paper flowers which they said somebody had sent me, and peered with lights into my eyes while I tried, under instruction, to tell one dusty blossom from another. They were very satisfied with the results. The next day I had a copy—I am not making this up—of "Peter Rabbit" in 36-point type. I recited it faultlessly, as indeed I had been able to do at the age of two, when I didn't know even one letter of the alphabet from another, but did know at which word the page ought to be turned. I wondered how many thousands of copies of that precise edition of the book they had bought—and when; had they been stocking "Peter Rabbit" against global war when I was two?

But luck gave them an accurate picture of my pro-gress. I could have recited the text in smaller type than that; they just did not ask me to try. Any idiot knows that the key line on the eye chart reads FELOPZD, if he's worn glasses from childhood, whether he can see it or not—but evidently the Department of Defence wasn't just any idiot. Had they brought me a letter in smaller type, I would have broken my heart trying to *read* that, and failed; but they knew better than that; they never brought me any letters, if indeed any were being sent me at Alert, and so I passed.

That was, evidently, good enough for them. The next day they dressed me in issue clothes and took me on a breath-taking elevator ride. I had really had no idea how deeply that hospital was dug into the rock until then. The elevator settled itself with infinitely slow caution when it reached its stop—like all hospital elevators, it was designed for surgical patients who must be rolled across the threshhold on their litters without any appreciable jar—but even before it nudged itself that last half-inch into true, I could hear the winds again, even through the doors of the cab. When they glided apart, the sound came in around me in a rush of thin turbulence. I felt cold all over again.

It was bright and cheerfully sterile up there, with many windows, all of them blank and brilliant with nascent sunlight illuminating nothing. The orderlies helped me—I was still throwing my foot a little where the invisible dog had cut a stabilizing muscle free of its attachment; they had saved the foot, but the muscle had withered before they'd been able to hook it up again. We walked down a short stretch of corridor into a roomful of people.

I recognized five of them, including Col. McKinley and his aide. Jayne was there, sitting with her ankles crossed and her hands folded in her lap, her face pale, composed, and without make-up. Across the room from me were Harry and Harriet, sitting close together. I could not see their expressions; my eyesight wasn't that good yet, especially since they had their backs to a blazing window; they were little more than silhouettes. Nevertheless, just the way they were sitting suggested fright, confusion, and a stubborn defiance. Also, they were holding hands, which did not require any interpretation; time and the ice had shown them the one way out.

"Good morning, Mr. Cole," Col. McKinley said. "Glad you're making such good progress. Please sit down. There are a few questions we'd like to ask."

I could see that, all right. McKinley and his aide were seated behind a long table, together with two Army officers wearing the insignia of the Attorney General's Corps, and two enlisted men running stenotype machines.

"This looks like a court martial," I said. "Either that, or you've got a unique notion of how to assemble a reception committee. Jayne, have you been allowed to see Harry and Harriet before now? Obviously they've been separated from each other."

Jayne shook her head. The Colonel tapped a pencil on the tabletop.

"Please, Mr. Cole," he said. "This is not a court martial. You know very well that we can't conduct legal proceedings against civilians. It's simply an informal board of inquiry. We communicated the bare facts of your arrival here to Washington, and they authorized us to proceed. Obviously it would be impossible to assemble a grand jury in this part of the world."

"What do you consider the bare facts?" I said. "To get such an authorization, you must have come damn close to rendering a true bill of murder while you were making the request!"

He leaned forward and looked at me with slowly blinking eyes; I could see them turning blank, dark, blank, dark.

"Well, Mr. Cole," he said coldly, "what would you call it? We brought back one severely mangled man with a crushed skull, and another with a fatal gunshot wound in the chest. The shot was fired point-blank. We also brought back the weapon, and a very simple series of checks showed that it was the one used in both cases. There are two members of your advance base crew that we can't account for at all, except by reference to your S.O.S. to Mr. Chain—which might have told the truth, and then again might not. I told Washington no more than that. Since your expedition was an official Air Force mission, it was quite sufficient, I assure you."

He tapped twice more with the pencil, and then added: "I could well have done a little reading between the lines, Mr. Cole. There is something about the North that makes a man forget where he came from. He feels isolated in a world of his own—as though anything that happens to him here has no reference at all to the out-side world. And mixed-sex expeditions have peculiar problems of their own, no matter where they happen to be exploring. I said none of this, but I had to consider it."

"I see," I said. "When you reported your simple checks, you didn't go into any advanced, highly technical details about the fingerprints on the rifle, I suppose."

He flushed slightly. "We checked the prints," he said. "Naturally."

"Before, or after?"

"After," he said curtly, leaning back in his chair.

"Sure. There's a right way, a wrong way, and an Army way—anywhere in the world. I see it also holds true for the Air Force. What did the prints show?"

He was silent for several seconds. Then he said:

"Well, Mr. Cole, suppose you tell me. You seem to think you're better qualified at legal procedures than we are."

"I don't know a tort from a tart," I said. "All I know is the press, and the law of libel, and the laws relating to invasion of privacy: that's required of every newsman down to the lowliest cub. If you radioed your request to Washington, we're being tried unofficially for murder in every paper in the United States, right now—unless, of course, you sent the request in code. Did you?"

He said nothing.

"I thought so; you sent it in clear. Evidently we're not the only ones who are a little detached from the outside world. Would you care to show me a copy of any newspaper you got in your most recent mail? No? Hell, man, you know less about law than I do, and I've already admitted I'm a total incompetent. As for those two shavetails with the Ay Gee lapel jewellery, they must be ambulance-chasers nobody wanted back stateside."

Both the second lieutenants stiffened and bristled; so did McKinley's aide.

"You'd better watch your language," the aide said in a high, clear, unpleasantly penetrating voice. "You don't seem to realize——"

McKinley flagged him down; the Colonel seemed to be repressing something perilously close to a sour smile.

"These officers," he said, "happen to be experts in international law. We couldn't operate up here without them, as I'm sure you'll appreciate."

"I'll give them that. All the same, if this were a civil action I'd have them up to their necks in malpractice suits by tomorrow morning. Now I'll answer your question. You found no prints on the Parkchester but Elvers'. And your serology lab right here in the hospital was able to identify what was left of Elvers by blood-typing, and gastric analysis of the dead dogs; you're in no doubt about what happened to him. In fact, you've been unable to shake our account of what happened in any particular whatsoever, and you're pumping us now in a last desperate hope of salvaging a colossal blunder. Go on, deny it."

"I deny it," Col. McKinley said, his face wooden once more.

"Harry, have they been grilling you about this?"

"Twice a day," Harry said, grimacing.

"Harriet?"

"Me too."

"Fine," I said. "Colonel McKinley, you know yourself that neither of these two kids were in our advance camp, and couldn't stand up as anything but hearsay witnesses for ten seconds. They couldn't know anything that we hadn't told them by radio—which you would have intercepted, just as you overheard our call for help before Harry relayed it. So any questions you asked them represented the worst kind of a forlorn hope. You've been tormenting them solely to save your next promotion—which looks mighty remote right now. Let's hear you deny that."

"For an incompetent, you're a remarkably adept prosecutor," McKinley said. His face, normally red from constant exposure, was mottled with lobster-coloured patches.

"I'm a human being, God damn it," I said savagely. "I wouldn't be surprised if your Public Information Officer didn't put you up to this. From his point of view it must have been a sensational break, and to hell with the suffering it would cause. Is that right?"

"Lieutenant Church asked for permission to send out a release," McKinley said expressionlessly. "I suppose it's possible that he influenced my thinking. The responsibility for the decision, however, is entirely mine."

I had to admire him for that, furious though I was. McKinley's record, as I found out later, is clean; he had never been in a position to bring off anything spectacularly heroic, but he is one of those unimaginative, workhorse career officers who hold the armed services together between heroes. His admission redoubled my conviction that he had been booby-trapped by some staff underlings intent on pulling a coup.

"Lieutenant Church never stopped to think that one of his pawns was a newspaperman," I said. "Or maybe he didn't know that the Air Force Information Services are quite open about showing their manuals and other P.I.O. directives to accredited reporters, especially those on science beats. I seem to remember that A.F.M. One-Ninety dash Four defines 'sensationalism and exaggeration' as *Not Releasable*. The same goes for 'terminology or phraseology tending to convict the accused in advance trial'—I remember that one verbatim because of the typo, the omitted 'of' before the last word. Would you like to show me his release? You might as well; after all, it's in the public domain now."

McKinley nodded slightly to his aide, who was wearing an expression not far removed from open hatred. With a last glare at me, the man got up and left.

I was sure of my grounds now. For a while there, especially at the start, I had only been shadow-boxing. I got up. The orderlies stumbled after me, but I'd caught them by surprise. I was standing beside Harry and Harriet before they could catch up with me; I stared at them until they went away.

Harry looked up at me without making any attempt to suppress his grin. Harriet's eyes, however, were full of tears.

"Great, by God," Harry said under his breath. "I thought we were in a hell of a spot until now. Geoffrey knew what he was doing when he hired you on, Julian."

"No, he didn't," I said in a low voice. "He had no eye for people at all, or he'd have left me home. And we *are* in a hell of a spot. Getting out from under this phony grand jury is child's play—but we're already ruined back home. Harriet especially. McKinley's ignorance is going to cost you your whole damn career up to now, carrot-top. No agency will sign you on after this, let alone an industry p.r. department. You know that, don't you?"

Harriet nodded. "I don't care," she said, almost inaudibly. She did not seem to dare raising her voice above a whisper. "It was my own fault. If I'd stuck to Geoffrey, maybe it wouldn't have happened. But at least I'm alive.

But Julian, what about you? Your reputation, your family——"

"One mountain at a time," I said. "You two are in love, aren't you?"

The tears came running down Harriet's cheeks. She reached out both of her hands for mine.

"No, Harriet, it doesn't hurt me. I do love you, and I wish I'd known it before. But, forgive me, I love two other women, too. Harry, it's true, isn't it?"

"Yes," he said gruffly.

"All right. I'm satisfied. Stick to it; you'll need it."

I disengaged Harriet's hands as gently as I could and turned away. The wind behind them rose desolately. With care, I walked to Jayne; I had been facing the light so long that the centre of the room was almost blotted out by floating purple-and-gold rectangles. By the time I found her, my bad foot was hurting abominably, and so I got down on that knee, more or less necessarily. The officers behind me rustled their papers busily; in my heart I thanked them and forgot them in a split second.

"Jayne, are you——"

"I'm all right, Julian," she said. "Never mind. I heard what you said to the kids. That's enough."

"No, it isn't," I said doggedly. "There's——"

She put a cold hand over my mouth. "Shh," she said. "It's quite enough. Thank you, and God bless you. Between Geoffrey and you, I won't need another man ever, I think. Let's let it rest at that."

I got helplessly to my feet. Behind me, Col. McKinley cleared his throat, and I turned reluctantly. The aide was back, and McKinley was holding out to me a sheet of legal-length mimeo paper with grey writing on it. I looked at it without really knowing what I was seeing.

"The release," McKinley said, with peculiar gentleness.

"Oh." I thought about it. At last I said, "I think I'll waive that, Colonel. Thanks for offering it to me. But I'm not mad at Lieutenant Church any more. I think maybe we'd just better all be allowed to go home."

McKinley lowered the release slowly to the tabletop.

"As you wish," he said, spacing the words evenly, without emphasis. "If I can help you, Mr. Cole, I hope you will say so. I think we owe it to you."

"You can help Mrs. Farnsworth, and the kids," I said. I was suddenly very tired. "Not me. I did kill Commodore Farnsworth, Colonel; also, I killed Dr. Wentz. Not with bullets or blows, no. What I did wasn't actionable. But I'm the man, and your stenotypists should so enter it."

"Julian!" Jayne cried out.

"I think not," Col. McKinley said. "As a matter of fact, our typists here are only students, here for practice. I will review their transcripts very closely; they probably contain many errors."

He stood up—very stiff, very military. "This board is adjourned. Captain, instruct Lieutenant Church to prepare an appropriate release for my inspection. Then schedule a flight out for tomorrow. Assign pilots for the expedition's planes, and ship all the expedition's salvageable equipment aboard them, on consignment to Mrs. Farnsworth; we will send the snowmobiles out by the next Navy freighter. Route the survivors to the Air Force base closest to their preferred destination."

"Yessir," the aide said, scribbling furiously.

"Dismissed."

I turned, stumbling. *But 'twas a famous victory.* I looked back as the orderlies took my arms, and saw Harry and Harriet still sitting side by side, clinging to each other's hands. The wind was rising again around the hospital. Any moment now, it seemed, it would carry them away.

We were met at Stewart Field—for after all, despite Col. McKinley's good intentions about our "preferred destinations", we none of us had any place left to go but New York—by a huge Unwelcoming Committee of reporters, photographers, radiomen, newsreel and television cameramen, and sightseers. Nobody from the public relations departments of our sponsors put in an appearance, of course. Midge wasn't there either, but I had anticipated that—in fact, I was responsible for it: the first thing I had done after Col. McKinley had dismissed us was to get his permission to send a radiogram, warning her that my arrival time was uncertain and that I would see her at home the instant I could make it. The last thing in the world that I wanted was to greet her in the middle of a wolf-pack. I would have recognized her— my eyesight was now almost as good as new, I had to give the Air Force surgeons that—but I was none too sure that she would recognize me.

We had all anticipated it, and while we were still in flight, Harriet had suggested that we get off the plane scrambled—me first, as a figure of some public interest; then Harry, who would be skipped impatiently by the Unwelcoming Committee; then Jayne, who would be photographed in batteries no matter where in the order she fell; and as an anticlimax, Harriet, who would stay behind to parry the questions. It was ingenious, but I was stubbornly opposed to it. I wanted us to disembark as human beings, not as pieces of a newspaper story, and in particular in such a way that Harry and Harriet weren't separated. I suggested instead that Jayne go first, as the surviving officer of the expedition, followed by Harry and Harriet, the last working members. I didn't care where I fell, as long as it was on the ground; last was as good as any place.

But as it turned out, it wouldn't have made a bit of difference in what order we got off the plane. It was Jayne they wanted, and it was Jayne they got, despite the half-hearted efforts of the field's military police— who after all had no reason to suspect the pushing civilians of any hostile intent. My attempts to spoil their shots only resulted in their getting several pictures of Jayne and me together, which of course was one of the things they most wanted.

In some other respects they did not make out well at all. Jayne was hollow-cheeked, sunken-eyed, and still without make-up; a good many newspaper readers were going to find it hard to believe that she was Jayne Wynn, even with "before" portraits for comparison. Nor would she, nor any of the rest of us, say anything but "No comment". We said it over and over again, scores of times at least, and at long last we managed to bore the boys—otherwise we might be there still.

On the train to Pelham I had a chance to see what the first editions did with the story. It was not pretty reading. Furthermore, there were so many holes in the background material that I suspected—accurately, as I found later—

that we had already been in the papers for a good many consecutive days.

The story that I read did include about half the text of Lieutenant Church's release, which was a model as retractions and exonerations go—I could see Col. McKinley's hand in several of its key phrases—but of course such things never make as good copy as the original allegations do. The Church handout was hooked to the jump of the story, as a three-em shirt-tail. The jump, of course, was on page 36, back with the horoscope and Little Orphan Annie.

Midge was on the phone in the hallway when I opened the front door. She slammed the handset into its cradle unceremoniously and ran when she saw me. She ran my way.

In that instant, I knew that I was home.

"Julian, Julian," she crooned when she got her breath back. "My God, I was terrified. Are you all right? Are you really all right?"

"I'm fine," I said shakily. "I had all kinds of luck. Where are the kids?"

"Out in the park. I didn't want them here, not yet. My God, I still can't believe it."

I held her tighter, and we didn't say anything for a while.

Finally I said huskily, "Let's have a drink to celebrate. I've got to sit down or I'll fall down. It's hot in here."

"No it isn't. It's just right."

We sat down on the living room couch. I had already forgotten the drink.

I looked around.

"It's different."

"I moved some furniture. It gave me something to think about."

"Who was on the phone?"

"The L.-C. They want your own true life story, by-line and all. Ten instalments, ten thousand bucks."

"They're mighty free with the old man's money now that he's dead," I said. "Speaking of which, who's president now?"

"We don't know yet. The hospital isn't talking."

"Oh? He's sick again?"

"That's what they say." She looked at me. "Julian—"

"That's me."

"No it isn't," she said, and burst into tears.

I held her and waited. There is never anything else that you can do.

"It's me," I insisted gently, when I thought she could hear me. "Midge, it's all right. I'm not hurt, and I didn't shoot anybody, and everything's going to be all right, and the L.-C. can go drown in its own filth for all I care."

"I don't care about the goddam L.-C.," she sobbed, clinging to me. "Except for the kids. You should hear what gets said to them. Oh, Julian, Julian, what happened? Is it true about that bitch? Was it all good for anything?"

"What happened was simple and very ugly," I said sombrely. "We lost some of our party on the first day out, an unnecessary accident. Another man, one of the best we had, died of pneumonia. And we had a madman among the survivors; he killed Geoffrey, and Fred Klein, and would have killed Jayne too if the dogs hadn't turned on him."

She was looking at me strangely, her eyes wet.

"And is that all?" she said in a level voice.

"It's all that I know for sure, Midge. If you mean Jayne, she's no bitch—and I probably did sleep with her. I'm not sure about it, but I hope I did. I turned her down once when I shouldn't have. If I failed her the second time, on the last night, I was a zombie without a drop of compassion in my whole body. I only hope it isn't so."

"Because she'd lost her husband?" Midge said.

"Because she had lost him years ago."

She crossed her hands on her knees and looked at them for a long time. Then, without looking back at me, she said:

"I'll get the drinks."

She went into the kitchen. I found that I couldn't sit still. I got up and walked around the room, touching things. On the mantel above the fireplace, my book on tracer medicine was open to the hard chapter, *Operation REScue*, the one about Dr. Snell's basic research on the reticulo-endothelial system.

It takes a whole history to know what will move a man deeply at any instant in his life. Until my return to Ellesmere, I had not been able to cry since childhood, when I realized that I would never be spanked again after the day I failed to howl about it; but I gained nothing by so crippling myself—nowadays my nose runs instead, which is even more undignified for a grown man. That open book made me snivel as no Polar wind had been able to do. In it I could see Midge, who was bored by the simplest scientific matters, trying to reach me through the nearest thing she could find to my voice, no matter how dull, no matter how remote from the world as she saw it.

I picked up the book and went back to the couch with

it, where I sat turning the pages in a kind of stupor. What comfort could she have gotten from all that stuff about the molybdenum fraction of xanthine oxidase, the potentiation of micrococcal toxicity by mucin, the carbon-14 labelling of metabolic precursors in reticulocyte generation. . . . What comfort had anybody been able to get from it, for that matter? It was only magic.

I heard Midge's toe strike the kick-plate of the swinging door between the dining-room and the kitchen, and then she came in with a jingling glass in each hand. It had taken her a long time to prepare two simple highballs; her eyes were quite red. But she was not crying now.

She came into the living room and sat down quietly on the floor, leaning against my legs. I took a glass from her. The Scotch smelled good, and though I thought of Joe Wentz as I lifted it, it tasted good too.

"I thought about it," Midge said huskily. "And I was right: it isn't you any longer. You never used to notice other people enough to know what they needed, most of the time. That answers the other question I asked."

"What question?"

"Whether anything good came out of it all. I—I'm glad you slept with Jayne. I'm glad you went. It's going to be hard to get used to, living with another man. But I think I'll like it. A touch of adultery helps make Suburbia go around."

"It's not another man," I said, baffled. "It's just only me, Midge."

She turned and leaned her arms across my knees. She was wearing her gamin grin.

"Don't tell me," she said. "And I won't tell anybody

else. As far as I'm concerned, you're an impostor—but it's a secret between us. Wait till we go to bed tonight. You're going to have your work cut out for you; my husband hasn't been officially reported dead yet."

And then she burst into tears all over again. I leaned over and kissed the back of her head. I was far from sure that I knew what she was talking about, but I was content to wait. I could hear the four girls coming up the walk.

The telephone was hardly silent a minute. It was easy enough to shuck off the newspapers; they were still getting nothing out of Jayne, and Harry and Harriet's marriage gave them something new to write about which drew their attention further away from the expedition rather than closer to it, although I'm sure that's not the way they thought about it. Neither bride nor groom told them anything either; and when Jayne gave them half of her salvage money, they vanished, on a honeymoon to some place the reporters were unable to trace. (Only, I suppose, because by that time the whole subject was running rather thin, so the reporters had given up trying really hard.)

The other calls were harder to take. Most of them were from colleagues in the science-writing racket. Their questions were penetrating and hard to parry; their commiserations were even worse. Almost uniformly they wanted to know what I was going to do for a living now —which of course I couldn't answer except by telling the truth, which was none of their business—and What the Hell Really Happened, Anyhow, Julian?—which I couldn't answer either. Hardest of all to take was the universal assumption that I was passing them on the way *down* that mountain.

I could not argue that; furthermore, I didn't want to. I had already been to see Ham and Ellen Bloch. From then on, my erstwhile colleagues were plucking at the wrong bleeding tree.

"What the hell really happened, anyhow, Julian?" Ham said, pouring me a tall Pilsner glass. "I went over your man Wentz's figures a dozen times, and I couldn't find a thing wrong with them. I had a hard time convincing the IGY, even with Ellen to help, but I wasn't in any doubt about it myself. Wentz accurately reported an unbelievable event—that's what it seems to come down to. But can you go on from there?"

"No," I said. "I have a theory, Ham, but I'm bound not to tell it. Maybe sometime later—but I can't promise even that."

Ham sat down by Ellen and leaned forward earnestly. Over his shoulder, I could see the plate of the meson explosion in his wife's office; it made him look as though he were wearing a star-cluster for an epaulet.

"Are you in trouble, old scout? There's been a lot of loose talk. The Artz books are by the board—you know that. Not even Ellen could rescue them now. We know; we tried."

"You shouldn't have," I said, my nose filling. "The whole Second Western Polar Basin Expedition was a preposterous fiasco, and I couldn't possibly write any book about it anyhow. I just have nothing to say that anybody would believe—let alone anything of any scientific merit to report."

"As bad as that?" Ellen said.

"Just that bad."

"*I'd* believe you," Ham said gently. "Julian, if you can't trust me, who can you trust? I am your friend. If you tell me not to say a word to anyone else, I'll obey completely. But I would like to know what it was all about."

I thought about it, turning the Pilsner glass in my hands. I had thought about it before, and nothing new occurred to me now.

"Ham," I said, "I'll tell you before I tell anyone else. And that's as far as I can go. I'm not concealing any crime, except perhaps in the historical sense—and don't ask me to explain my qualification. I'm not in trouble with myself. I'm not holding out anything that the IGY ought to know—or at least I think I'm not. I'll promise this, too: if another satellite disappears, then I'll open up right away. But I can't now. I am the only man left in the world who can choose to speak or to keep silent about this, because I'm the only man left who saw— what I saw. And I choose to keep silent, for what I think are good reasons. I can't say anything else."

Ham lit a cigarette, and watched the smoke rise judiciously.

"You are also the only man in the world," he said suddenly, "who could satisfy me with that answer. Ellen, what do you think?"

She only smiled at him. I will never forget that smile.

"I owe you something," Ham added, as though there were some connection. "Do you want a job? I'm thinking of chucking the university—it's up to its ears in weapons development anyhow—and going into the instrument business. I could use a writer—somebody who could write

217

specifications and manuals on the one side, and sales fliers and advertising on the other. I couldn't afford two men, but one man who could do both jobs would take a big load off my back. And you could advise me on trends; I'm too specialized to watch them, most of the time."

Ham had invented his instrument business right there on the spot. If I hadn't already known him well enough to suspect it on my own, one look at Ellen's expression would have convinced me.

"Thanks. No," I said huskily. "I don't want to be in the instrument business, at least not on the producing end. I've got too many other things to think about."

"But Julian," Ellen said. "You must be rather short of money."

"I'm a little short. It doesn't worry me; I'm running too large a plant, that's all. I've known it for years, but this is the first time I've gotten up the courage to do something about it. Ham, you could help me there, I think."

He inclined his head attentively. I took a deep breath.

"I'm going into astrophysics," I said. "I'll have to go back to school. I can keep myself and the Pelham crew alive—we'll sell the house for a starter—but I can't cover the tuition. Could you help me get a scholarship?"

"Julian, you crazy Apostate bastard!" Ham said, his eyes glittering. "Of course I can. How is your calculus? Never mind, I'll teach you that myself; it's easy. Do you know what you're getting into? You couldn't make it into a graduate school, Julian. You'll have to start 'way back—maybe even as a freshman. Some of it may have to be done nights. I can bung you into Tech like a shot, but after that it'll take years of work on your part—maybe ten years. Are you *sure*?"

"I'm sure," I said steadily. "I'm all through with the second-hand stuff, Ham. I want the real thing. I'm starting all over again. That's how it's going to be."

Ellen got up. "Excuse me," she said, with great dignity. "I am going to cry." She vanished into her office.

Ham's eyes were like furnaces. "Have you told Midge?" he said.

"No, not yet. First I wanted to hear what you would say. You could have said that I hadn't the talent."

"Every man," Dr. Hamilton C. Bloch said to me, "is born with a talent for the truth. It's not his fault if the people around him teach him to hate and fear it. But it *is* his fault if he likes it that way, and teaches it to his children. If Midge doesn't see it that way, you send her to me, and by God I'll tell her it's so."

"No, Ham," I said. "I'll tell her. I'd better go and do it right now. I'm sorry I upset Ellen——"

"You're a crazy man," Ham said gruffly, standing up. "Ellen was way ahead of me. She'll never forgive you, and neither will I. You say you're starting all over again. How many growing thirty-six-year-old boys do you know that that's happened to? Great God, man, *don't you know that we envy you*?"

No, I hadn't known; and I was not sure why they should. Even from the top of the mountain, it looked like a long road still ahead. But I put my first foot down on it across Ham's and Ellen's doorsill, on the way back to Pelham, and somehow I was in no doubt whatsoever that tomorrow—though that be only the next day after today, or the end of the world—I would be walking among the stars.

XV

I waited a long time to break silence, even to Ham, and I thought I had good reason, just as I'd told him at the beginning. The reason had nothing to do with the fact that I could hardly have gotten anybody to listen to me during the first years. In the fullness of time, Jayne had after all found a third man to love, a man who had been silently in love with her for God knows how many years —young Faber himself; it was the last headline she ever made. I could easily have broken what I had to say through the Faber chain, had I felt urgent enough about it to risk bringing her back into a limelight she no longer either wanted or needed. Or, I might have risked Ham's reputation; his endorsement, not necessarily of what I had to say, but of my credibility, would have made news all by itself, and insured me an audience among the science writers at the very minimum.

But I kept silent, because throughout those years I was unable to convince myself completely that Elvers had indeed been only a crazy man who ran about on the Arctic ice-cap in shorts, and thought he was better with dogs than he turned out to be in the pinch. Each time I would settle uneasily back on to that comfortable conclusion, a sharp point came out of it and nipped me.

Most of the stings were small, but their effects were cumulative. Out of Elvers' "legend" about the destruction of Nferetet and Infteret, for instance, I remembered that Elvers said the Martian atmosphere had been thinned, until the high ice-clouds were as close as sixty miles from the ground. Sixty miles is a figure that, as a chiropodist whose madness had taken a form suggested by Geoffrey, he would have had to have plucked out of nowhere at random. Yet it happens to be the precise depth of the Martian atmosphere today, as ultra-violet photography shows it. He got the figure from Geoffrey? No, because Geoffrey rounded figures, Elvers never did. Geoffrey placed the diameter of Ceres at about five hundred miles; Elvers said that the moon of Nferetet was 480 miles in diameter, which happens to be—if "happens to be" really summarizes the situation—the *precise* diameter of Ceres.

In Elvers' "legend", there were two asteroidal proto-planets involved, not counting Ceres. From the point of view of celestial mechanics, two is the minimum number. Geoffrey, the protoplanet bluff, hadn't known this; how could a chiropodist have hit upon it? For that matter, I have checked the dynamics of such a system, and I've asked another man to check *me*; in particular, I asked my expert at what date two such planets would naturally collide. He placed the date at "about a million years from now, give or take ten thousand." The agreement with Elvers' date is good; Elvers' is just slightly outside my expert's margin of error.

(And don't take my figures for it. My expert is the only expert there is on this subject; if you know the subject, you'll know just where to find his name in the preceding pages. If you don't, I have no intention of attaching that very eminent name to so irresponsible a series of speculations as I am engaged in here. I am speaking alone, to myself and for myself.)

Elvers was an adult albino. Human albinoes are doomed creatures who must stay out of the sun as much as possible. When they must venture outside, they have to wear clothing which covers as much of their bodies as possible, and their hands and faces must be coated with a carefully calculated equivalent of sun-tan oil, which screens out every scrap of ultra-violet light from the sunlight that reaches their skin. If they don't observe these precautions scrupulously, they die in childhood, of cancer of the skin.

Elvers never took any such precautions. As Geoffrey had pointed out to me, even a normally pigmented man would have risked severe sunburn in the togs which Elvers wore at the Pole. What does this mean, except to prove further that the man was insane? I don't know; but every time I thought of Elvers walking bare-legged and bare-armed under the Polar sun, I remembered that on Mars the sun gives far less heat than it does here on Earth, yet is far fiercer on the UV end of the spectrum because of the thinner air. No albino could have survived there who carried the skin-cancer gene, as all Earthly albinoes do—and as Elvers, going by his behaviour alone, just as plainly did not.

Elvers knew what the copper dawn was, and had a most appropriate name for it. To this day I have yet to encounter any reference to it elsewhere, even in the most likely places. How could Saint-Exupéry have missed it, for instance? But evidently he did.

There is a fair arsenal of additional small-shot I could bring into play here, but this is not a text. I could, I think, make just as good a case for the other side—that Elvers was not and could not have been a Martian. The oxygen tension on Mars appears to be too low to support any animal life above the level of a worm, let alone as complicated an organism as Elvers was. Similarly, Elvers was water-based, as we all are; how did he survive dehydration in an atmosphere as poor in water as Mars' is? It is easier to see how he might have survived freezing—he knew how the Eskimos take shelter and husband heat—but no animal with normal lungs can breathe air which contains no trace of water vapour without being killed by it. And if Elvers was evolved to breathe the atmosphere of Mars, how could he stand our water-heavy air even at the Pole, let alone in muggy New York or Washington? And if he was so different from humankind that he did not breathe at all—after all, we have no autopsy, nor have I been able to run down any record of any physical examination he ever had in his life—then where did he get his energy? He could hardly have been a plant; there are all kinds of fundamental, ineluctable arguments against an autotrophic man.

But I never found any record of his birth, or of his past, until he turned up in the Bureau of Standards in 1950. The government's habit of secrecy has protected his application papers and back-file from me; but where was he before he worked for the government? An adult albino ought to be a medical prodigy, fully documented in the literature—especially since the way to protect them against cancer sufficiently to allow them to grow into adulthood wasn't discovered until two years *after* Elvers went to work to Washington.

And, of course, there was the Lump.

I have no final answer, though I have been muttering in my beard about it for years. Last month, however, President Kennedy announced that the First Fleet will leave SV-2, the second manned satellite, for Mars sometime within the next six months. The science writers fumed; they hadn't been told that any such fleet was a-building. I wish I had known about it earlier myself, but I've worked as fast as I could to get this all down: the story of the Second Western Polar Basin Expedition, as it happened, by the man whose duty it was to record it.

If Elvers was not, after all, insane, then the First Fleet may have a nasty shock awaiting it when it sets down on the Sinus Roris.

But, on the whole, I think it won't. Whether Elvers was mad or sane is almost beside the point. I do not think it will be Martians who will bring us to the end of our tether; if we all die, next year or in a million years (give or take ten thousand), it will be by our own hands. Elvers was mad, but that did not make him imported; his madness was familiar.

If you suppose that he was just what he claimed to be, the answer is still the same. I think we will die by our own hands; I am certain that Elvers' Martians are impotent to kill us. They can have no real idea of what they're up against; men are not what Elvers—or Julian Cole—thought they were. They might, in fact, even let Elvers' people live.

And you could call that revenge, if you like.